Esther's GOLD

A Novel by

SHIRLEY E. SCHMIDT

To Joan

Shirley E. Schmidt

Order this book online at www.trafford.com/08-0907
or email orders@trafford.com

Most Trafford titles are also available at major online book retailers.

Artwork/Design: KoubaGraphics, Inc.

Cover Photographer: Lacey Stiller at Shuttering Memories Photography

Note for Librarians: A cataloguing record for this book is available from Library
and Archives Canada at www.collectionscanada.ca/amicus/index-e.html

Printed in Victoria, BC, Canada.

ISBN: 978-1-4251-8309-7

*We at Trafford believe that it is the responsibility of us all, as both individuals
and corporations, to make choices that are environmentally and socially sound.
You, in turn, are supporting this responsible conduct each time you purchase a
Trafford book, or make use of our publishing services. To find out how you are
helping, please visit www.trafford.com/responsiblepublishing.html*

*Our mission is to efficiently provide the world's finest, most comprehensive
book publishing service, enabling every author to experience success.
To find out how to publish your book, your way, and have it available
worldwide, visit us online at www.trafford.com/10510*

 www.trafford.com

North America & international
toll-free: 1 888 232 4444 (USA & Canada)
phone: 250 383 6864 ♦ fax: 250 383 6804 ♦ email: info@trafford.com

The United Kingdom & Europe
phone: +44 (0)1865 487 395 ♦ local rate: 0845 230 9601
facsimile: +44 (0)1865 481 507 ♦ email: info.uk@trafford.com

10 9 8 7 6 5 4 3

CONTENTS

Thank you
to all who helped me put this story into print.

A special thanks
to my grand-niece Rachel
for posing as Esther on the cover.

1

GROWING GIRL

THE WOOD FRAME SCHOOL HAD A DECEPTIVE LOOK of somber quiet about it that day in 1845. The whitewash had eroded to various shades of grey. Those who do that type of work know that fresh whitewash would be applied soon, now that the weather is warmer.

The older boys were the first to leave the one story school, as they burst from the door and down the steps as though chased by a demon. The spring air seemed to energize them for horseplay as some of the boys tossed a ball back and forth while two of them tried to intercept it.

Three girls walked out of the building together and down the wooden steps, stopping to look at each other as they talked. They are pretty young girls. Their high buttoned shoes are barely visible below their long skirts as they descend the stairs in a most ladylike fashion. Esther's long honey colored hair shone in the sun as it was blown by the wind. She walked away from the others, going another direction. Her preteen figure was just a bit chubby with the signs of young womanhood just beginning to show. She breathed in the fresh warm air as she looked up at the tree tops. The light green leaves were just peeking out as they prepared to receive the summer sun.

Sarah, a girl with brown hair and a bright blue bonnet, called to her, "Some of us are going to watch the boys play a new game called baseball. Do you want to come?"

Esther's face was immediately serious, "I have to help my mother work at the hotel."

The boys' horseplay had brought them close enough to hear the conversation. Harris, the tallest boy with carrot red hair, called out, "We all know what that means! She's gonna carry shit! Have fun carrying shit pots, Esther!"

Esther remembered that Harris was staring at her one day when she was emptying the chamber pots in the back of the hotel. Harris was right. Her job was carrying the chamber pots from each of the occupied rooms, and replacing them with the ones that she cleaned earlier. She took the full ones to be dumped into a barrel on the garbage wagon. The wagon was then driven out of the city to be dumped. She hated the stench, but it had to be done each afternoon after school. "Do you want to come help me? We could get the job done faster if you helped."

"I wouldn't take a job like that!" Harris had a look of utter disgust on his face.

Sarah and Leah entered into the banter, "Leave her alone, Harris!" they called out, almost in unison.

Harris continued in spite of the other girls coming to her defense, "Why is it ya hafta work, anyways? Yer only a school girl! …. Oh, it's because you don't have a father! You probably never had a father!"

"Everyone has a father!" Leah called out.

Esther was planning to ignore the taunting, but she was really angered by his lies. "You know my father is dead!" she called out.

"Why has nobody seen him, then? He doesn't even have a grave."

"He was buried at sea," Esther said firmly.

"Your mother wasn't married! Yer a **bastard**!" Harris called out loud enough for the whole town to hear.

The girls all gasped at the last declaration, and the other boys suddenly stopped their play to stare. Harris reveled in the attention, so he said it, again. "Yer a **bastard**!"

Esther's face reddened, more with anger than embarrassment. She wanted to turn and run, but she thought everyone would believe Harris if she did. "I am not!" she screamed, "My father died on the ship."

"That's what cher mother tol' ya, but ya don' know it's true."

When Esther heard that, she ran. Her long skirt made running difficult, but she wanted to put distance between her and the terrible lies. She heard some noise behind her, but she didn't want to look back to see what was going on. She tried to stop the tears from coming, but it was not possible, so she continued to run.

She ran as fast as she could until she was past the crest of the hill and in the grove of trees, then she returned to a more ladylike gait. She was accustomed to walking at a pace that gave her as much speed as possible without losing decorum. Her mother and the Harbor Hotel owners, Mr. and Mrs. Knutson, had taught her to behave in a ladylike manner at all times. Running inside the hotel was not allowed at any time. Esther pulled a hanky out of her pocket to dry her tears as she slowed to a walk on the path through the wooded area. She was glad that her mother always insisted she carry a hanky. She believed her face was in good order by the time she walked down the knoll and out of the cover of trees. She carefully crossed the busy street.

Esther remembered her mother telling her that the hotel was originally built outside of Boston, where it was quieter for the guests. As the city grew, the hotel was now on the edge of the city. She was wishing the street were not so busy today. She felt everyone was looking at her tear-stained face so she walked without looking to either side.

The heels of her shoes made a louder clunking sound than usual as she strode onto the wooden sidewalk and into the front door of the hotel. Mr. Olson was at the desk. His balding head was turned down to look at his work on the desk. As he looked up, his blue eyes seemed to take over his thin face and he smiled at her, as he usually did when he heard her coming. She liked to walk into the front door of the hotel when she returned from school. For a few seconds she could pretend she was going to be a guest in the hotel instead of a chamber maid.

Esther walked up the stairs toward the back hall where she and her mother shared a room. In the hall, she met a family making their way to the stairs. A young girl about her own age spoke to her. "What room are you in?"

The question took Esther by surprise. "I live in a back room," she said.

"You live here all the time?" the girl asked.

"Yes, I work here," Esther said.

"But you get to stay here, in this hotel! You are so lucky!"

Esther smiled. She thought of inviting the girl to help her with the work, but she knew she couldn't do that. The girl's parents told her to come along, so Esther didn't have to reply.

The room where Esther and her mother lived had been planned for storage at one time, so there were shelves in the room and one small crude table they used for a desk. There was one window to let in light, high on the wall opposite the door. Esther would sometimes take their one chair and stand on it so she could look out the window, although the view of the sky was usually better than looking at the alley below.

The rooms for the guests had varnished wood paneling, but their room had been whitewashed over rough boards. By the small stove in the corner there was a light coating of soot on the wall. Mr. Knutson would provide whitewash to lighten things up, but there had been no time to clean the wall and apply it.

Esther looked into the small mirror hung on the wall to check her face as she hurried to change to her maid's uniform. She pinned her hair up on top of her head and pushed it into the lace trimmed round cap that matched her green uniform. Her hands were larger, and her arms were longer and more muscular than her friends.

She wanted to start the hated job so she would get it done for the day. On Saturdays and Sundays she could help in the kitchen when her clothes were clean. The smell from the chamber pots seemed to cling to her, so she was not allowed to work in the kitchen after doing that job.

Some days she stopped by the kitchen before she started work after school, because Mrs. Knutson would have a snack for her. Mr. Knutson once said, "Vat! You are giving the help our best dessert?" Mrs. Knutson got very indignant as she told him, "Sometimes I make a mistake, so some don't come out so gud, ya. Esther is a good girl; she helps me get rid of my mistakes!" Mr. Knutson grumbled under his breath as he walked away, but Esther noticed a small grin on his face. Today, Esther did not feel like eating. Even the Scandinavian pastries didn't tempt her.

As Esther started working, her mother came up to her in the upstairs hall. "What's wrong?" her mother said as soon as she saw her up close. Her mother's slightly darker hair was also under the same style of cap. Mother and daughter looked alike, especially about their blue eyes, but Esther's face was softened with rounded cheeks.

"One of the boys at school was calling me names," Esther said quietly. She was not even surprised that her mother had noticed her mood. It had happened too many times. Esther didn't realize that the usual sparkle would leave her face when she was upset.

"That doesn't usually bother you," her mother observed, as she knew that drunken guests had called both of them names in the past.

"I know, but he called me a bastard."

The two continued working as Esther's mother, Millie, thought with a furrowed brow. After a few minutes she said, "I didn't realize till now that nearly all of the people that sailed over in the ship with us have moved on. I'll talk to Mrs. Kinnen. Maybe she will talk about your father's sickness and death on the voyage to some people in town.

"Her son is the one who is calling me a bastard!" Esther exclaimed in a hoarse whisper.

After a surprised look, Millie got quiet. "We'll talk in the room, later," she finally said.

Hotel guests were in the hall, so the two talked of which rooms were occupied. Esther was glad that her mother was helping with the work that she usually did alone. She knew that her mother also worked very hard each day while she was in school. At times, all fifteen rooms were full.

When Esther was finished with the required work, she brought water to their room, so she could wash up for supper. She was early due to her mother's help, so she did some of her homework while waiting for her mother to have supper with her. Supper was usually leftovers, or an unpopular item from the menu.

When Millie walked in, she went to a shelf and pulled down a wooden box. She placed it carefully on the small table where Esther was working. "This is all I have left of your father's things." Esther watched as her mother fingered a belt, a man's handkerchief, a watch and several other small things. "Here is the letter the captain of the ship wrote about the burial at sea."

Millie spoke seriously, "That captain didn't want me to return to England with the ship because I was with child. He didn't say anything, but he said that since I couldn't be dependable on the return trip, I couldn't sail as a worker. The captain asked for double the rate we paid to come over. I was desperate. I was ready to go begging from house to house, asking for someone to take me in. I was crying in the hotel dining room. Kara Knutson noticed my tears and asked me to tell her why I was crying. When Kara heard my story, she told me that I would be needed, because they were planning to add on to the hotel. She said she likes to cook, so I could do the cleaning. After you were born, you slept in the kitchen. Kara would call to me when you were hungry. They never told me that they were helping me. They always said **they needed** me."

Esther looked at the letter. "Mama, you don't have to prove anything to me. I know you didn't lie to me, but I wish Harris could see this."

Millie put everything back in the box. "This is really none of Harris' business. I'm going to tell you about Harris. I am telling you about him, because I want you to know about all people that call out names, or make others feel bad in any way. First, you must promise not tell anyone what you know."

"I want to slap him silly, but he's bigger than me."

"Pretend he is smaller than you. Would slapping him make him your friend?"

"Why would I want **him** for a friend?"

Millie sighed, then said, "Let's put it another way. Would he stop behaving that way?"

"No. He'd just pick on someone smaller. I promise not to tell anyone, ever."

"Harris **is** the same thing he called you."

Esther's mouth flew open. "But . . . . his father is the captain of a ship."

Millie continued, "His mother sailed with your father and me. Her family paid her way to America in the hopes that she would find a man here, in spite of her shame. Harris was two years old. On the way over, she and Mr. Kinnen fell in love. He wasn't a captain, then. The captain of the ship married them. Most people thought she lost her first husband. I lived near her in the old country. Talk was that she kept company with a married man. He may have paid her to leave before people could see the family resemblance. She asked me to keep her secret. I never told anyone. Most of the passengers moved on, so Harris is now believed to be Mr. Kinnen's child."

"She always acts as if she thinks she is better than everyone. She acts so self important when she shows off all that pretty china and things her husband brings for her."

Millie nodded, knowingly. "Harris was probably called that name he had for you."

"You said nobody knows."

"The man Harris knows as his father might be the one."

"Mama, that's awful!"

"Yes. You will not make your life better if you tell anyone. Hold your head high, knowing that a person who calls you names, probably feels less than you in some way. You don't have to defend yourself in any way that makes Harris' mother and everyone feel bad."

"I won't, Mama. I won't ever talk about it." Silently, Esther prepared herself for seeing Harris the next day. Everything inside her wanted to kick him with her words, as he had done to her. At the hotel, she always had to mind her tongue. Guests were to be treated politely no matter how bad their manners. Now she learned that she must not speak her mind at school.

Again, Millie sensed her daughter's uneasy feelings. "God will take care of Harris," she said. "God knows what a wonderful girl you are. He also knows what a wonderful woman you will be."

At school the next day, Esther looked around the room. Harris was conspicuously missing from the area where the older boys sat.

The teacher began to speak in an unusually somber tone. "It has been brought to my attention that there was a fight after school, yesterday. Harris was injured in this fight. His mother has asked me to speak to the boys responsible. Since Harris will not name the boys that attacked him, I will speak to all of you. Fighting is against the rules. Anyone found to be using violence on the school grounds will be sent to the school board for discipline. This may mean expulsion."

Esther noticed that as the teacher spoke, some of the boys looked in her direction. Esther saw the teacher follow their gaze. She wanted to shrink down in her seat, but she purposefully held her head high. *I didn't do anything wrong. I didn't ask the boys to beat up Harris. He deserved a beating, but I didn't cause it.*

One of the younger children raised his hand, "Why would there be an explosion?"

The teacher went to the blackboard and wrote the word, *expulsion.* "Do we have a volunteer to help Sam look up this word?"

After school, Esther sought out her friends. "What happened after I left last night?"

Sarah looked about to be sure no one could hear. "All the boys piled on Harris. He didn't have a chance to get in a hit. It wasn't just you. He's been after the other boys all year. It was just too much to see him starting on the younger girls."

Leah nodded in agreement. "Harris' mother told my mother that Harris is getting to the age when he needs a father to handle him. His father is gone to sea, now."

As the girls continued to talk, the minister walked into the school. The girls stared and wondered aloud at his reason for being there. The school had been used as a church in the past, but the church had been a separate building for years.

Leah asked, "Do you think he could be sweet on the teacher?" The girls giggled, and then got serious as they realized the minister had a very somber look about him.

Reluctantly, the girls separated to go to their homes.

Esther was met by her mother when she arrived at their room. "Esther, I wanted to tell you what has happened, so you won't be so surprised by it if you hear it while we are working. Harris' father died suddenly at sea."

"Mama, did you know that the other boys beat up Harris after I left school yesterday?"

"Yes, I saw him. His face was swollen. His mother said he is bruised all over. We didn't talk much about it. He hid in a back room as soon as he saw me. I think he expected me to tell his mother the reason for the beating. I didn't think Mary Kinnen needed to deal with that now. I made a condolence call. That's all that was needed."

"Was Harris' father buried at sea?"

"Yes, he was. Why do you ask that?"

"Harris was calling out that my father didn't have a grave."

"I hope you don't think this happened to avenge what he said."

"No, but it does seem like his own words came back at him, seven times over."

"I can't believe you are only twelve years old."

"I'll be thirteen next month!"

"Just the same, you seem older than your years. You have seen so much, working here with me. Speaking of work, we have to get some work done."

"We do?" Esther said facetiously.

"We'll get time off to go to the memorial service. It will be at the school, tomorrow."

2

ATTACK!

IT WAS A LOVELY SUMMER DAY. ESTHER WORKED quickly, as she planned to go riding with her friend, Leah, in the afternoon. Just as she carried the last two pots, a guest called out to her.

"My dear lady, I could use your help in here, please." The young man was dressed only in his under shorts and an undershirt. His skinny legs were bowed from spending a lot of time on horseback.

"I'll be back as soon as I empty these," Esther promised. *I have to ask Mr. Knutson to be here. I always get another person when a man wants me to go into his room, and this one isn't dressed. I have an uneasy feeling about his syrupy sweet talk.*

"My chamber pot is full and I want it out of here, now!" the man demanded. "It's stinkin' up the whole room!" The half dressed man came forward with his hand outstretched to grab her arm. Esther moved out of the way of his grasp as she was taught to do. Guests were not to touch her.

Esther decided to put down the full pots, so she was not able to avoid the man's grasp the second time. He put his arms around her waist and easily picked her up. Esther was not allowed to disturb the guests by talking loud, but she knew this was an exception. She screamed before the man could cover her mouth. She knew he would harm her if he got her into the room. He was holding her arms so she put out her legs as far as possible when they approached the door. She was hoping to prevent him from carrying her into the room, but when her left heel hit the door jam with force, the pain caused her to pull back. The man could not cover her mouth and control her appendages at the same time, so she was able to scream, "Help me!" before he put her into the room.

The man threw Esther onto the bed and hit her on the face.

"You keep quiet, bitch!" he said.

When he turned to close the door, Millie had arrived and held it open. Millie screamed, "We need help here, now!"

When the desk clerk, Mr. Olson, arrived the two women were wrestling with the young man, but they were losing. Mr. Olson's slight frame made some progress by controlling one arm. Soon Mr. Knutson's stocky frame filled the door.

"Vat is dis?!" he yelled, as he put a large arm around the man's neck. "Ya vill be letting loose, now, or your neck will be loose from your head."

Esther felt the man go limp. She stood free with her clothes askew. Her hat was hanging on by one pin. The two women stood ready to act, but they were no longer needed as Mr. Knutson guided the half dressed man out.

"You can't throw me out like this!" he yelled.

"You would like for to be missing some parts, now?" Mr. Knutson countered.

"My clothes! I'm not dressed. Let me get dressed!"

"Mr. Werner, Ya din' have need of clothes when you took hold o' my chamber maids. Ya don' need the clothes when yer hide hits da street." Mr. Olson silently followed down the hall. He rarely left his desk, so he returned to it now.

Esther knew she should get the dirty chamber pots out of the hall, but she could not trust herself to pick them up. Her arms were too shaky. Slowly, she began to feel pain. Still, she looked out the window to watch as Mr. Knutson picked up her attacker by his underwear and literally threw him onto the gravel street with his shorts torn half off.

Mr. Knutson gazed up and down the street till he saw Mr. Gibbs, the sheriff. A gesture told the sheriff that he could take over from there. Mr. Gibbs tended to arrest people that were not properly dressed in public.

Mr. Werner was escorted down the street toward the jail, limping and bleeding from abrasions, as he held his shorts up with one hand.

Esther could no longer see them, so she turned and checked the pot in the room. It was clean, just as she thought it would be. She found one of her hairpins on the floor. She used the mirror on the vanity to look at her face. She put her hair back up and replaced her cap. Her face was red and swollen on the left side.

When Esther moved to pick up the pots in the hall, her mother stopped her. "I'll get these. Go wash that face in cold water to help with the pain."

Esther didn't want to touch her face, but she obediently took a cloth and a pitcher of cold water to their room. She could imagine what it might be like to go riding with Leah in the sun. They would slowly ride sidesaddle until they were out of sight. She could almost feel the wind in her hair as she would put one leg over the saddle and urge the horse to a gallop. *Do I dare ask to go?. ... Yes, I'll ask. I need to get out of this hotel for a while and go!*

Esther's mother came in with her most concerned look. "How are you doing?"

"I hurt a lot."

"I just want to tell you that you did nothing wrong. I can tell you were just carrying those pots down the hall when that man forced you into the room. That's what worries me. If I had been farther away, he might have gotten the door closed. It would have been a longer time before we found you."

Millie slowly shook her head. "I hate to think of it. Maybe I should have married one of those men that proposed to me. You shouldn't be exposed to the men coming in from the wilderness where they live by their own rules."

"I wouldn't have Mr. Knutson to protect me somewhere else. You shouldn't have to marry someone you don't love. I'll never let that happen to me, again. I will learn to protect myself!"

Esther backed away as her mother moved to hug her. "I'm too sore," she explained.

"Just lie on the bed awhile. You need to heal." Millie's eyes were tearful.

"I would rather go riding with Leah. I want some fresh air."

"How will you explain your face?"

"You said I didn't do anything wrong. What's wrong with the truth?"

"I don't have to explain what that man was planning to do to you. It's wrong, I know, but people tend to blame a woman for enticing a man in these situations."

"I didn't entice him to do anything. I was carrying the chamber pots down the hall."

"You know what that man had in his mind. We have talked of this."

Esther said, "It's wrong to blame me for that man's horrible behavior. I still want to go riding with Leah. If I stay cooped up in here, I'm being punished. I want to show everyone that I'm a free woman, not a criminal."

"You are just a young girl. Go riding, then. I understand why you feel the need for fresh air."

When Leah came to the hotel, riding one horse and leading the other, Esther was ready to go. Leah's light brown hair was braided, but free of the bonnet that was tied to her saddle horn.

Mr. Knutson was standing by, reluctant to see her go, but he merely said, "You go to the kitchen so all of us talk after the ride."

"What's wrong with your face?" Leah asked as soon as she looked at Esther. Her blue eyes were full of concern.

"I'll explain on the ride," Esther told her.

When they were alone, Esther told her friend the facts of what happened without telling the implications.

"Was he planning to rape you?" Leah asked.

Esther nodded. "Yes, he probably had that in mind, but I didn't think you knew that word."

"I know that word. Farm girls learn a lot, too. Just don't tell my parents that I know that word. I'd probably be locked in my room."

The girls took a trail too narrow for riding side by side, so they talked little till they reached Leah's home.

"Your home is so beautiful!" Esther told Leah. She admired the porch with tall columns that reached up to the second story. As they walked past the large rooms, Esther noticed beautiful furniture in each room. The rooms in the house were as nice as the guest rooms of the hotel. There was even a room devoted to books. "You have your own library!" Esther said. When Esther had visited another time, she had gone directly into the kitchen, so she was enjoying the tour.

"I read in the kitchen by the stove when it's cold out, because the library is so cold. Now I can read in my room when my chores are done."

Esther went to the window in Leah's room. She could see the cleared pastures with cows and horses grazing lazily. *I want a view like that from my window, someday.*

Leah's mother called up the stairs, "Leah! You had better not be sitting on your bed with those horsy clothes!"

"We're not! Esther just wanted to see my room."

"You girls come down to the kitchen for a cool drink of lemonade."

Esther followed Leah's example and washed her hands in the basin of water provided. She was accustomed to getting her own water. When they sat at the table, Leah's mother, Ida Durham, waited on them, giving them glasses filled with lemonade and setting a plate of cookies on the table.

"Whatever did you do to your face?" Leah's mother asked.

"A man at the hotel hit her for no reason," Leah answered quickly. "The sheriff locked him up in jail."

Ida gasped as she sat and studied the bruising. "I can't believe your mother lets you near such a man!"

"Nobody knew him," Esther told her. "He just rode in last night."

"Leah, you stay away from that hotel!" Ida ordered.

"Mr. Knutson saved me at the hotel. If a man like him rode in here, who would save us?"

"Such impertinence! Young lady, you should learn to mind your tongue!"

"I'm sorry if I sounded impertinent, Mrs. Durham." Esther said quickly. "I just know that Mr. Knutson works very hard at keeping the hotel safe. I have seen men offer him double the money to allow them to continue to stay there, but he refused. He told them it was important to him to keep a hotel for families, not rabble rousers."

"Well, at least you have been taught to apologize when your tongue gets away from you." Mrs. Durham went about the kitchen working on one thing, then another. Her jaw was set and she said no more. Esther could tell she was angry.

Esther and Leah finished their snack quietly and went out to the horses tied to the post by the front door.

Leah looked at Esther before they mounted and said, "I'm sorry my mother got so huffy. My parents are so protective, sometimes. They won't let me do anything on my own."

"My mother didn't want me to go riding. She thinks riding is a threat. Why don't our parents listen to us?"

"They think they know it all," Leah decided.

When they rode down the trail through the sugar maples, Esther called out, "It's a good thing I didn't tell your mother the whole conversation I overheard."

"I understand, but now you have to tell **me**."

"Mr. Knutson told the man to stay in the hotel across town. The man complained that his wife would leave him if she found out he stayed at the whore house. Mr. Knutson told him that if he brought his wife, he could stay at The Harbor Hotel, but until then, he wasn't welcome."

Leah giggled, "Yes, I'm glad you didn't tell her that. She doesn't think I know about places like that. I heard that Mr. Kinnen went there."

"No! How did you hear that?"

"I overheard my brothers talking in the barn when they didn't know I was there."

"Did they go there?"

"No. My dad would beat them silly if he caught them going in there. They were riding by and they saw him hand the reins to the groom and walk in. The groom told my brothers that Mr. Kinnen went there every time he was in port."

"I used to think Harris Kinnen was lucky to have such a nice home," Esther observed.

"Do you miss having a father?"

"Of course. I even wish I could remember him, but he died before I was born. I don't think my mother and I would have to work so hard if I had a father."

"I still have to work hard. Maybe not as hard as you do."

"If I had a father we could have a home. We stay in the back room of the hotel. We never leave work. I would give anything to have a home like yours with my own room."

"I never thought about it, before. Our house is a lot of work, but it is nice."

"Let's gallop!" Esther called, when they reached the road.

"Race you to the fork in the road!" Leah called, as she urged her horse on.

3

TRIALS WITHOUT A TRIAL

ESTHER REPORTED TO THE KITCHEN AS SOON AS she cleaned up a bit from the ride.

Kara Knutson hurried over to her as soon as she arrived. Kara stood three inches shorter than Esther. "Oooh, my little one!" she exclaimed as she gently moved a stray lock of hair from Esther's face. "Ira Knutson! You didn't tell me it was dis bad! Dat fool could have knocked her whole head off! Bring 'im here ta dis kitchen! I have some t'ings I want to use here! He won't have a hand to be a hittin' young girls, after dis!" Kara said as she brandished the largest cleaver in the kitchen.

"Simmer down, now, Kara. We can't get him out of jail just like dat. Esther, get your mother. Bring her to da big room upstairs now. We'll talk."

Kara did not lose her stern look of resolve. "Ira, you get a doctor here. She is going to hurt worse in da morning now ya know."

"A doctor too now?"

"A doctor," Kara repeated, sternly.

The four of them sat, in the hotel room. All were very quiet till Ira Knutson spoke. "I would take that scoundrel out to da bushes and fix him good, witout no help, but da law has say in dis, now. Most times da trouble makers are put outside town and told not ta show dare faces, again. Dis one is anudder ting now. Esther will sit and tell da sorry tale if he goes before dat judge. Vat do ya t'ink about dat now?"

Millie said, "I don't want Esther to have to go to court. I know what some people will say about her. The truth doesn't matter to them, they just talk. I don't want Esther hurt."

Esther looked at her mother, and then said, "I should tell the judge what this man did to me."

All were silent till a knock came at the door. It was the sheriff. He walked into the room, but said nothing. His tall frame moved toward Esther as he studied her, carefully.

His lined face was stationary, showing no emotion till he asked, "Mrs. Carter, this is your child? That piece of trash I have in jail did this to her?"

I'm not a child! Esther objected silently. *I don't feel like a child. I do a woman's work in a day.*

"Dats wat he did and more," Kara told him. "Da doctor will look at da bruises he put under her clothes."

"That's a good idea, Kara." The sheriff turned to Ira and said, "I'll have him before the judge in two days, before that face heals. If we let this one go, who knows who he'll get ahold of next?"

"Vat do ya say den, Millie?" Ira asked.

"If Esther is willing to go to court, I will not stop her. I just worry about how she will be treated."

"Da sheriff and I will take care of anybody dat does harm to our Esther, one at a time," Ira said, "Dis one first."

"Kara and I have to tend to business," Ira said reluctantly. "Esther, you will not be workin' till you heal. When you are better, you go to da kitchen. Kara needs help dare." Ira turned to Millie. "Mrs. Kinnen will be wit' you on da floor. She asked me for a job and it's my tinkin' she'll be comin' in da mornin'."

"Thank you, Mr. Knutson," Esther said. *I got beat up, but I get to work in the kitchen. Some good things come with the bad. Mrs. Kinnen has to work, now. That will be interesting. I wonder what Harris will think about his mother cleaning the chamber pots.*

The sheriff quietly told Esther that he had to hear the whole story from Esther and her mother separately, so everyone left while Esther told the story and answered questions.

The next morning, Esther woke before dawn. *Mrs. Knutson was right. I hurt worse, today.* The moonlight was bright enough to allow her to see her mother's sleeping form. She could hear her soft, slow breaths. *I don't want to wake her. She was sitting up till I went to sleep. I should go out back and use the outhouse. Oh, but the stairs! I don't think I can walk down the stairs!* Esther lay still for a time, but her need to urinate would not go away. *I have to go, so I'll move one part at a time. My legs hurt so bad! I'll grit my teeth and move!* She pushed herself up with her arms in spite of the pain. *It hurts so much to walk! I'll walk a bit here in the room. ... It's easier, now. I'll put on my housecoat and go to the outhouse. Maybe I could use the chamber pot, just this once. If I use a chamber pot, I'll have to clean it later. I don't want to do that. Maybe I'll never have to clean a chamber pot again. I'm a kitchen worker now.*

Carefully, Esther made her way out the back door by moonlight, and into the women's side of the outhouse. After she was relieved, she sat quietly steeling herself against the pain for the move back to the room. The sound of hushed voices convinced her to remain quiet. She didn't want to talk to anyone just now.

"This place is locked up," one voice said.

"We can break that window," a familiar voice said.

"Garret, we'll wake up the owners if we break in. Let's get out of here. If we're both in jail, who's gonna get us out?"

"I need to get that bastard! He threw me onto the street like a dog."

Esther put her hand over her own mouth to stifle a gasp as she realized her attacker was only a few feet away. She controlled her breathing to remain as quiet as possible. *The door from the hotel to the outhouse is open. They must have tried the kitchen door.*

"He'll throw you back in jail, that's what he'll do."

"I have a gun!"

"He's got a gun, too, and he knows this place. Garret, we're leaving now. I want no part of killin', and I don't want to be shot or hanged."

"I could take the girl."

"You're not thinkin'. Didn't you learn anything? You have to go through all those other people to get that girl. There's lots of other girls. Better girls than that one. I'm leaving this town!"

After a short pause, Esther heard a horse begin to move away.

"Wait up, you chicken livered bastard!"

I'm dead if I move too soon. I have to wake up Mr. Knutson! Did they hurt the sheriff?

As the second horse moved away, Esther stayed quiet to listen. She could hear only the usual sound of the ocean and the sounds of the wind. *I'll make my move fast. Even if there's someone out there, I might be able to get inside before they catch me.* Carefully, Esther lifted the hook on the inside of the outhouse door and bolted for the hotel. When she got inside she walked toward the Knutsons' room behind the registration desk. The hall was very dark, but she knew her way very well. She felt for the door and knocked, waited, and then knocked harder while calling out in a stage whisper, "It's Esther! Wake up!"

"All right, all right den a'ready!" she heard Mr. Knutson's say.

He had a lamp, so he illuminated her face as he opened the door. "Esther, it is. Your mother is well, then?"

"Yes, but I went to the outhouse and I heard that man talking with another man."

"Vat man is dis, talking?"

Esther took a deep breath. "Another man broke the man that attacked me out of jail! He was talking about getting even with you and me, but the other man talked him out of it."

Kara joined her husband at the door. "Esther, go up to yer mother and lock da door, now. When Ira gets his pants on, he'll go to da jail."

Esther made her way up to the room. The moonlight was giving way to the light of dawn. Her mother was awake when Esther walked into the room.

Millie said, "Esther you must have eyes like a cat. I've told you so many times to take a lantern to the outhouse."

"This time it's a good thing I didn't. I'd be shot or kidnapped if I had a lantern with me." Esther slipped the bolt into place. "Mama, you won't believe what just happened!"

Esther put her housecoat away after telling her mother what she had heard. She slipped back under the covers, but she couldn't sleep. Mid morning a knock on the door woke Esther. She realized she had gone to sleep after all.

"It's Kara, Esther. I have news for you. Esther opened the door, and Kara walked in, saying, "Da news is not so gud. Da sheriff was hit on 'is head and robbed of 'is keys, so dat man is loose now. Da doctor will come here later for you, but now he is tending to Mr. Gibbs. He was hit hard. Da sheriff's men rode around da town to look for dose men, but dey are back already now. Da devils are gone."

"Oh, Mrs. Knutson, that man will be back! He said he wanted to get the man that threw him into the street and take the girl!" Esther got the words out quickly before the sobbing prevented talking.

"Men rode nort' and sout' to da law in all da towns. Dose sheriffs help each udder, ya know. Da men could still be caught, now. Don't cry, Esther, and it's time you start to call me Kara. We're like family, you and me, and you're such a big girl, now."

Esther bore the pain of the hug without complaint.

The doctor came as promised. He told Esther to get extra rest. When she had rested all she could, she dressed and went to the kitchen.

When Kara saw her, she said, "And vat is it you t'ink you'll be doing here?"

"I'll help you till I'm tired, and then I'll go rest."

"And you're a bit hungry, too, now?"

Kara put a plate of food on the table where the help ate. "Sit and eat, den we'll see what we do about da work." Esther ate carefully to avoid biting her swollen cheek.

Kara was busy with preparation for the supper crowd, so she had little time for watching Esther. When Esther finished her food, she noticed the fresh rolls were not prepared for the table, so she broke them apart, put them into the baskets and covered them with a cloth. At one point Kara noticed that Esther was helping get the orders out, but she was too busy to object.

When the rush was over, Kara shook her head at Esther, and said, "You're good help for me, but you should be upstairs resting."

"I feel safer down here with you and all these weapons." Esther told her. They smiled at each other. Esther winced from the pain of smiling.

A week later, Millie came into the kitchen with a well dressed woman. The woman carried white gloves and her blue summer dress was made from the finest cotton with lace trim. "Esther, Kara, this is Greta. Ira said it would be alright if I showed her around. She wanted to see the kitchen."

Esther was about to leave the kitchen for a break. She walked toward the woman and simply said, "Hello." The woman stared intently at Esther. The multicolored face was causing a few stares, so at first Esther didn't think it unusual. This woman was staring more intently than any stranger had before. Suddenly there were tears in Greta's eyes. Greta turned to hide the tears, but the other three couldn't help but see them. They looked quizzically at each other.

Kara said, "Come sit at da help's table. No woman can leave my kitchen wit da tears runnin' down."

Millie and Kara shared a knowing glance.

Greta gently took hold of Esther's hand and openly sobbed.

Esther looked at the woman's eyes. A small shiver went down her spine.

She was drawn to this woman and repulsed at the same time. Esther moved to the help's table and almost pushed the woman toward a chair.

"I'm so sorry, Esther," Greta said through her tears.

The three waited for the woman to explain the apology. Finally she spoke, between sobs. "Twenty years ago, I was attacked. . . . . I told no one. He was a rich man. . . . . He told me that no one would believe me. Then I was going to have a baby. . . . . I had no where to go. . . . . I stayed with the man that attacked me. He said he would care for me and the baby. . . . . He did care for me, but he beat me. . . . . I thought I could teach the baby to be a good man that does not beat women. I was so wrong! My son, Garret is the man who attacked you, Esther. I heard him tell his father about it. His father only told him that he was stupid to take a girl in a hotel where she is protected. My son left the house. He plans to go west to get away from the law. We will not see him again. Julius got money from the safe for Garret. For the first time Julius didn't notice I was watching. The next day, Julius took the wagon to town to replace the supplies Garret took with him. I took just enough money from the safe to get away, packed a horse, and left. All these years I slaved for that man. He never married me. I came to this town. He won't look for me here. I know if Julius finds me, he will kill me." Greta took a deep breath.

There was a thoughtful pause. Greta continued, "Now I need to find a place to stay that's not so public, and some way to make my living."

When Greta began to move from her chair, Kara said, "Sit still." in her commanding voice. Kara looked at Millie. "Ira's in da back showin' da new yard boy what to do. He'll come in, now."

Greta's eyes widened with fear.

Kara saw the fear and said, "Don't worry, my Ira is a kind man."

Greta said, "I don't know why I told you all of this. I just wanted to say how sorry I am, and the whole mess came spilling out. I'm sorry if I said too much in front of this child."

Millie looked straight at Greta and said, "God sent you here. Don't think any more about it. Esther has been here since she was born. She has heard and seen more than most. The three of us know how to keep things to ourselves, so just consider it a closed subject."

Ira came into the kitchen and sat at the table. "Aw right, awready, Kara tells me you are here to apologize now. There is no need for you to be apologizin' to any of us. If you are hopin' to live in dis town, dare is one t'ing that comes to mind. Da sheriff here in dis town is not tinkin too gud. He got hit on da head so hard, he got da learnin' knocked out of it. Da doctor is lookin' for a hard worker to see to da needs of Mr. Gibbs."

Greta looked from one person to another. After a pause, she asked, "Is this the man that my son's friend knocked out so he could free my son from jail?"

"Dat is da one. Can ya do dat one, ya?"

"I don't know, but I'll talk to the doctor. Maybe he will be willing to let me try."

"One more t'ing you must tell us, now," Ira said. "Tell us da name of your son's friend. Da one dat hit da sheriff. Where did 'e go, now, ya?"

"The friend, Duncan Eberly, went with my son. I only know that they went west to get away from the law."

Esther decided to keep her thoughts to herself. *She is such a beautiful woman. She has beautiful clothes. She looks like a rich woman without a care in the world.* Esther went outside to get some cold water from the pump. She was not allowed to use the ice delivered from the ice house since her face was healing. That was for guests of the hotel.

As time passed Esther was almost able to forget the attack. At least she didn't feel the fear all the time.

4

A WOMAN'S PLACE

IN THE FALL OF 1847, ESTHER WAS 15 years old. Her figure had lost the slight chubbiness that she had as a child. Her cheeks still had a fullness that gave her a healthy look. Her hair had darkened to a light brown. She didn't realize how beautiful she had become. Esther walked to the first day of school with a happy heart as she inwardly celebrated the freedom from the hard work in the heat of the hotel kitchen.

Leah's serious face instantly brightened when she saw Esther. "I was so worried you wouldn't come this year! I didn't want to be the only girl in our class!"

"I'm glad to see you, too. I haven't seen you in weeks," Esther said.

"My mother won't let me take you riding. She thinks I should only associate with other country girls. She says the city girls are exposed to too much filth and violence. The problem is that I don't know any country girls I can talk with. I talk about school and they talk about the work they have to do. They think I don't have to work in school."

"I'm glad your mother lets you come to the city to go to school," Esther said.

"I heard her tell my father that she didn't think you would be here."

"My mother said that I should work full time, but Mr. Knutson said that girls need education, too. He hired more help in the kitchen for Kara while I'm at school. I help with the supper crowd and make sure the kitchen is cleaned up and ready for morning."

"Who helps your mother? I hear Mrs. Kinnen is taking in sewing."

"Nan Russell helps my mother full time. Anna Shepard works in the kitchen helping Kara. Neither one is going to school this year. Their parents said there is no reason for a girl to go to school past the sixth grade."

"I heard Harris is a full time stable boy, now," Leah said. "He shovels horse manure. I heard him say, 'Yes, sir!' and 'Yes, ma'am!' I didn't think he knew how to be polite to anyone."

"Is there anything I can do to change your mother's mind about me? It's been two years since I was attacked. My mother warned me that some people would blame me, but I didn't believe it."

"My mother has a long memory. She won't say she hates you because that wouldn't be Christian, but she hates you because she thinks you are *too worldly*."

"Maybe my mother could talk to her," Esther said.

"I don't want to lose our friendship," Leah told her.

The school bell was ringing so dutifully, the girls went to class. After class, Leah hurried over to Esther. "When do you get time off work?"

"I have every other Sunday morning off so my mother and I can go to church. I also get Saturday afternoon off. I can get time off another day if I have a good reason."

"I have something in mind, but I don't know if it will work."

"Don't get yourself into trouble over me," Esther said.

"I won't!" Leah called, as she ran to get her horse from where he was staked out to graze during the day. Leah used a buggy to get to school. Some of the younger children would help her hitch up the horse so they could get a ride home on Leah's way out of town.

The next day, at school, Esther tried to get Leah to tell her what she had in mind, but she said, "I will tell you when I have it all arranged." On Friday, Leah told Esther, "Just be ready to go riding on Saturday."

When Saturday afternoon arrived, Esther took an older dress out of the closet. *This is good enough for riding. I wish I could have someone make dresses for me. It's so hard to get time to make my own.*

One of the dining room waiters knocked on the door and said, "Someone is waiting for you, downstairs."

"I'll be right down," Esther called out.

Esther hurried down the stairs, past the dining room, and out the front door. As she stood on the wooden sidewalk, she looked for Leah, but didn't see her. Leah's brother, Jacob, approached her.

"I hear there is a lady here who wants to go riding, but doesn't have a horse."

Esther stared blankly at the handsome young man. He removed his hat to reveal dark brown hair. She saw that he brought the same horse and buggy that Leah used. He smiled broadly, and said, "Leah is forbidden to come to the hotel to pick you up, but our mother did not say I couldn't take you for a ride. Leah will meet us at the target range. I want to practice for the competition next month."

Ira Knutson came out of the front door of the hotel. He stood between Esther and Jacob and asked, "Do I hear that you are asking ta take dis young lady away wit'out a chaperone?" His voice rose in pitch even more drastically at the end of his sentence.

Jacob looked at Esther, and then stood as tall as he could in an effort to look the tall man in the eyes, and said, "Yes sir, with your permission, I plan to take her to meet my sister at the target range, so they have a chance to visit. I'm sorry that I didn't think about the need of a chaperone, so I didn't plan for one."

"Dis is not proper! Esther, your mother knows about dis ride?"

"I did get her permission to go for a ride, but I didn't know Leah's brother would pick me up. Leah arranged it." Esther lowered her voice so as not to be heard by everyone walking nearby. "You see, Leah's mother doesn't think I am proper company for her daughter, so she told Leah she can't come to pick me up. That's why her brother came."

Ira's eyes widened, then narrowed as he said, "I don't like dis sneaking. Ya, but for Esther to be here on her time off is not right now, eider. The two of you come in and sit a bit." Jacob tied the horse to the hitching post, and the two of them stepped inside and sat on the plush chairs in the lobby as they were asked to do.

Esther blushed as some of the hotel guests looked their way.

Jacob broke the silence as he said, "I did want to get to know you, and so I was glad when Leah asked me to pick you up. I hope you will be able to go with me, but Mr. Knutson is right. We need to do things properly. We can't be leaving town without a chaperone."

Someone thinks I am a grown woman. Even Ira must think so or he wouldn't think I need a chaperone. I haven't seen Jacob this close since he left school after the eighth grade. He has pretty blue eyes. He also has a nice smile.

"I'd be happy to ride with you," Esther said quietly.

Ira and Millie approached. Millie asked, "Do you want to go with this young man?"

"Yes, mama, I would like to go if someone can go with us."

Ira said, "Well, den it's to be. I have da boys working on da firewood, so I will be in da buggy wit' da young people."

Millie smiled wistfully as she gave Esther a hug.

The buggy listed to one side as Ira stepped up to get into the back seat. He started talking when they began to move and didn't stop.

Esther sat smiling at the suddenly talkative man. *It's almost like having a father. I think he is enjoying this outing. He doesn't get away from the hotel very often.*

Leah was waiting at the target range. Esther wanted to stay with Jacob, but she went for a walk with Leah. "Why did Mr. Knutson come along?" Leah asked when they got out of earshot.

"Young couples do not go off without a chaperone."

"But you aren't. . . . . Oh, I guess it looks like that. . . . . Do you, ...well do you think about my brother that way?"

"I don't know, but I think maybe I would like to spend some time with him so I can find out."

"I wonder if I will lose a friend to my brother."

"Leah, we will always be friends."

"I've seen some girls that were friends in school, but when one of them gets a beau, they are separated. .... Go ahead and let my brother come calling. I want to see what my mother does when she finds out. Jacob has always been her *perfect little man*. She has been encouraging him to get a girlfriend." Leah and Esther both laughed.

"Maybe he won't ask to come calling," Esther wondered.

"Now that I think about it, I think he will. I didn't notice at the time, but he agreed to my plan awfully fast."

When the girls got back to the target range, they watched for a few minutes, and then Esther asked, "Could I try? I'd like to see if I can hit the target."

Jacob said, "I don't see why not. This rifle is ready to fire. Hold it steady and line up the sights on the target."

"You mean that little stick in the middle of that shock of straw?"

"That's the one, but be prepared for the kick the gun gives you."

"I've heard about that."

"Gently squeeze the trigger without moving the gun away from the target."

Esther flinched after the gun was fired, because of the noise. The stick of wood moved out of the shock of straw. "That's not so hard," Esther said.

Jacob and Mr. Knutson stared at the target with open mouths. They walked to look at it.

"She hit it straight in da middle!" Ira exclaimed. "She should shoot in da competition, ya?"

"It looks like a good idea," Jacob agreed. "She has a steady hand."

I had to have a steady hand to lift those chamber pots up over the edge of the barrel. If I didn't have a steady hand, I'd have the contents all over me.

"I need some cotton for my ear, though. It's still ringing," Esther observed.

The day of the contest, Jacob came to pick up Esther as planned. He was allowed to walk into the kitchen. Esther was in the middle of serving dinner. When she looked up, she said, "I'm sorry Jacob. I can't go out today. Mrs. Knutson is ill. There is no one else here that knows the work in the kitchen."

Ira walked into the kitchen with an armload of stove wood. "Today, the work has to be done. You'll come another day then, ya?"

Jacob's expression told Esther that he was as disappointed as she was. "Esther, I will let you know through my sister when I can come again."

Esther took time out to watch Jacob leave. When he was gone, it was back to the attempt at keeping up with the orders from the dining room. Esther noticed that Ira was watching her. "I am not as efficient as Kara," she told him. "She fills the plates as fast as the orders come in." *I shouldn't be angry with Kara. She can't help being sick. They wouldn't let me enter the contest, but I wanted to at least watch it. I want to see both Leah and Jacob. The breeze felt so good when I stepped outside. It's so hot in here.*

Why did Kara have to be sick today?

Ira said, "We have more hungry ones coming off'a da street. Kara needs more help in dis kitchen."

The next day, Esther got up before dawn to get ready to make breakfast. *At least there won't be so many people this early, she thought. The early yard boy will have the fire going. Hot cakes are easier than dinners. How has Kara done it all these years? She makes all that food and still has time to make desserts.*

Esther looked at the empty kitchen, suddenly realizing she did not know exactly how to make the batter for the hot cakes. Ira came in, followed by the new yard boy. *This isn't a boy, Esther thought. He's almost as tall as Ira, but he is so skinny. He is half as wide as Ira, and his skin looks too big for him. His clothes are so ragged. They look as though they will fall off him.*

Esther nodded at the new employee, but was in a hurry to ask the needed question. "Ira, is Kara feeling better this morning? I need to ask about her recipe for hot cakes. I know which ingredients to use, but I don't know how much."

The new yard boy spoke up in a thick Irish brogue, "I might be helpin' with the makin' of Sunday breakfast. Since I was a wee lad I helped in the kitchen of me father's inn."

Ira looked at the young man in disbelief. "My Kara is not well, so I won't have her t'ink we have any trouble brewin' in dis kitchen. Young man, go brush the wood chips off. Ya, and wash up at da pump."

When the young man came back into the kitchen, he was wearing one of Ira's shirts. He looked cleaner, but the shirt was too big for him. Ira followed him in and said, "You do what Esther tells you, ya? If she tells you leave, you leave, ya?"

Esther could not believe what she heard. She had always taken orders. Now she was the boss of the kitchen? She soon noticed the young man was true to his word. He needed to be shown the location of things, but he soon learned the flow of putting out the food. There was no break between the breakfast crowd and the dinner crowd. When Ira brought in the freshly killed spring chickens, they worked quickly to prepare them for dinner.

When the crowd was finally thinning out, Esther looked at the young man and said, "What is your name? We have been working together for hours, and I don't even know your name."

"My name is Darby O'Halloran and it is pleased that I am know you, Esther. Sorry I am to be so familiar, but I have heard no other name."

"My proper name is Carter, but Esther is what I answer to in this kitchen."

"Then Esther it is," Darby said as he turned to greet Ira. "Mr. Knutson, would it be too much to ask if I could take some of the leftover hot cakes to me baby brother. He has work, but he'll not be expectin' pay for another week. He'll be a starvin' by then, he will."

Ira raised his voice, "Hot cakes! I should say not!" Darby's face was crestfallen. "A growing boy can't live on a few hot cakes! You'll take along some meat and potatoes, too, ya? Esther, see that there's a proper meal for him!"

As Esther helped put some food on a plate, Darby asked, "Why is the Norwegian so nice to me brother? He hasn't laid eyes on 'im."

"That's the way the Knutsons are. They helped my mother when she had nowhere to turn after my father died."

After a thoughtful silence, Darby said, "I lost me mother and me father. I have an older brother back in Ireland. There's hard times in Ireland, there is. Me brother told us to leave his place. 'There's too many mouths to feed,' said he. We went on a ship with a promise of money when we docked in Canada. In Canada there was no money and no work for us. They called us the filthy Irish, they did. Many were sick. The two of us were healthy enough, so we walked and begged for work. In this place, some call us the filthy Irish, but I'm happy to stay where I'll be workin' for me feed."

"Your own brother made you leave?"

"I can't be blamin' 'im. He had his own to think about."

"Wasn't it your home, too?"

"Not at all, when the parents are gone, the son born first owns the all of it."

"That doesn't seem fair."

"Fair or not, that's the way it is on the Green Isle."

The next day, Esther went off to school, as usual. Darby and Anna Shepard were working in the kitchen.

At the end of the week, Esther sought out her mother when she returned from school. "Mama, I am so worried about Kara. When I return from school, she is up and working on some baking. She still gives up her food if she eats very much at a time. If she stands by the stove, she complains the smell of the cooking bothers her. Anna tells me Kara is so sick in the morning, she is retching before she eats anything. Mama, what can be wrong? Will you help me convince her to see the doctor?"

"You are talking about our Kara? You're sure of this?"

"Yes, mama, she is not getting better."

Millie finished placing the towels in the empty room. "Nan, I'll leave the floor, now. I'll be gone for a few minutes, so stay outside when you empty those chamber pots. I'll let you know when I'm ready to come back here."

Esther put her slate and books for school in their room. By the time she put on an apron and got to the kitchen, her mother and Kara were nowhere in sight. Anna looked at Esther and asked, "Could we take a short break outside? We're so hot."

"Where is Kara?"

"She went to the living quarters with your mother."

"You'll have to go one at a time, or wait till I get back." Esther made her way toward the living quarters. She knocked on the closed door. She heard some soft sobbing. Millie came to the door, and said, "Tell Ira that Kara needs to talk to him." Millie walked on out.

"Mama!? What's wrong?"

Millie continued to walk as she said, "Just get Ira for Kara. Kara will be fine."

Esther told Ira as she was instructed. Ira hurried through the kitchen toward the living area. His eyes were full of concern. Esther told the others to take their break, and started working on supper.

Esther worried as she and Darby worked together. The supper crowd was heavier than usual for a Friday evening. As she took the rolls out of the oven she wondered if Kara would be baking rolls again.

Two hours later, Ira came through the kitchen. Esther had never seen that look on his face. Esther asked, "How is Kara?"

"My Kara will be fine," Ira said. "The doctor was here. He said we have to give her some time to rest. My Kara is the best wife a man could have."

Esther saw tears in Ira's eyes, but he had a smile on his face. *What is happening? I have never seen Ira like this. I have never known Kara like this.*

Ira came in to help clean the large pans as usual. He had a knowing smile on his face, but he said nothing about Kara.

Kara was sitting at the help's table, eating a small roll as they finished the cleaning. Darby was almost out the door when Ira called him back. "Young man, I would like a talk wit' you."

Darby asked quickly, "My work is what you like?"

"Gud work, and gud cookin'. You and your brudder sleep in da stable?"

Darby nodded.

"I'll pay a month's rent for a room for the both of you. I'll give ya a letter to take to da store for some proper clothes for you and your brudder, too, ya? I ask you to work for me, here."

"I will be indentured?"

"No, I will still pay you, but we will have an understanding between two men. My Kara needs her rest. You will stay and work for us. I will pay your rent and five dollars a week. You will not be leaving ta work for anyone else for two years."

"I am not a fool, so I will be taking your kind offer. As God gives me strength, I agree to be workin' for you for two years. May God give us both good health and fortune." Darby stood up and shook Ira's hand.

"The dawn will see me here," Darby called out as he left.

Esther did not dare ask again about Kara's health. She sat by Kara with a cup of coffee. She seldom drank coffee so late at night, but she wanted to see if Kara would tell her something, now that everyone was gone.

Kara smiled weakly as she said, "Esther, you have been our only child all dese years, ya? God has seen fit to give Ira and me a child of our own, now."

Esther could say nothing till Kara touched her hand, and then she said, "Kara, that is so wonderful! A baby?"

"At my age, I thought it was the change coming early. When your mother came to me, she said I act like I will be a mother. The doctor said this happens sometimes to da women my age. Can you believe it, Esther? I am carrying da first child at my age?"

"It's a wonderful miracle, that's what it is!" Esther told her.

"Ya, I know it," Kara said.

On the way up to her room, Esther smiled at her own thoughts. *Kara is not deathly ill. She will have a baby! That look on Ira's face was pride. Darby is paid more than Mama and me. That's not fair, but it's the way it is. Men are valued more than women. Some people may call him a filthy Irishman, but he gets more money for his work because he's a man. Ira could have told me that I must stay in the kitchen full time, but he hired Darby, so I can go to school. That is good.*

5

THE TELLING GIFT

IN THE EARLY SPRING OF 1849, ESTHER WAS seventeen years of age. Jacob came to visit Esther on a rainy, sleety afternoon. There weren't many places for the courting couple to go when it was cold and raining. Ira refused to be a part of driving around town in the damp cold. There was a small sitting area off the dining room where they were allowed to spend time between meals.

Jacob had a package with him. The package was much too large to be a ring. When they arrived in the sitting room, Jacob handed Esther the package and smiled as he said, "This should be yours, anyway."

Esther opened the box to discover what she had suspected from the size and shape of the box. "Jacob! It's the new colt dragoon you won at the shooting contest last fall! Why do you say it should be mine?"

"You are a good markswoman, but they wouldn't allow you to enter the contest, because it was for gentlemen only. We practiced together all those months, and your shooting was as good as mine. I decided that I had to win for both of us. I'm used to a rifle, but this will work for you. You need some protection."

"Jacob, this is not an ordinary pistol. It's one of the new revolvers. This must mean that you want me to go with you."

"I do, but Ira and your mother won't let me take you across town without a chaperone. What makes you think they'll let you go to California?"

"You know the answer to that, Jacob."

"Esther, I want to marry you, but I want to go to California. Everyone says there is gold there, but the best mines will be taken if a man doesn't get there soon. We could make a fortune, Elliot and I. After my fortune is made, you and I could be married. Would you wait for me?"

"I will make no such promise! I want to be with **you.** If you go to California, I may never hear from you, again!"

"Of course you would hear from me. I give you my word."

"You might be killed by Indians. How would you let me know?"

"If you go with me, you will be in danger. The trail to California is hard."

"The work here is very hard. Riding to California is not easy, but I would rather be with you. Do you want to be with me?"

"Esther, I want to take you in my arms this moment. I haven't even been able to steal a kiss."

"You also know the answer to that one."

"If we are engaged, we might be allowed some time alone for kissing. You said that you will not honor a promise to marry while I go to California."

"If you were leaving by ship, I would be able to get word by return ship that you arrived at your destination. Riding west, there is no way that I would know where you are or if you are still alive. I can't live like that. It would break my heart."

"I promise to return for you. I don't want to put you through the hard trip to California."

"It seems to me that we are talking in circles. I will accept your gift, only because it means you care for me. I hope to take it on the trip west." Esther got up to leave the area.

"Esther, don't leave! I will ask Ira and your mother for your hand. I'll talk to Elliot. He says a woman will slow us down. I can't buy an engagement ring for you, because Elliot and I agreed to save all our money for the supplies and traveling money we need for the trip."

Esther sat near Jacob and took his hand. "You know that I don't need to show off an engagement ring. You can buy lots of things for me when we have our own gold mine."

Jacob smiled at her confidence. "What do you want me to buy for you?"

"Jacob, I have never had a home of my own. My mother and I have a room to live in. I want a nice home more than anything." Esther's eyes got a faraway look. "When I go into our home, I want to do the work that needs to be done as I see it. I don't want to see to the needs of thirty people. I want to see to the needs of the two of us. I want to look out of a glass window and see fields with cows and horses grazing, not a dirty alley."

"Esther, I will be the man that gives you that home," Jacob promised.

"I want you to be the man that I care for in that home."

People were beginning to gather in the dining room, so Esther took her hand away from Jacob's hand. Any public display of affection was frowned upon.

"Jacob, did you ever tell your mother that you were calling on me?"

"My mother knows. She told me that she understood why I must sew some wild oats, but that it was time I found a 'proper' girl. I have told her that you are very proper, but I don't think she believes me."

"Your mother has never liked me. I wish I could change that, but she is just one more reason we should leave this area after we are married."

"You are right about that. I will ask for your hand, tomorrow after church. When the wedding plans are set, we'll tell your mother and mine about our travel plans."

"I don't think we have to tell them anything about California. Everyone knows. Ira is looking at us," Esther observed. "I think he is saying that your visit needs to end."

"Do you promise me a kiss if they give us permission to marry?"

"I promise. I'll kiss you every chance I get," Esther whispered. She watched Jacob as he went out the front door.

Esther picked up the gift and went to clean the room that she shared with her mother. There was so little time to take care of their space. Because of the rain, she couldn't go to the washroom to wash her dresses. She washed some small things that could be hung in the room. She dreamed of caring for her own home. She dreamed of feeling Jacob's strong arms around her and the long awaited kiss.

When Millie came into the room, she saw the gun in its holster and asked, "Whose gun is that?"

"It's the gun Jacob won at the shooting contest last fall. He gave it to me."

"I expected he would give you a ring, not a gun."

"This gun is more valuable than a ring."

"Do you mean it costs more than a diamond?"

"He gave me the one thing he worked more than a year to win. He plans to ask for my hand tomorrow. He said he would ask you and Ira. What will you say?"

Millie gave her daughter a hug. "I should have seen this coming. You are too young! Stay with me one more year. Jacob will still be there. You have the opportunity to graduate from high school if you just go one more year."

"At school, I spend time with things like sewing that sampler that is hanging on the wall. I have trouble finding the time to make myself a dress, so I can look nice while going to school. I wanted to study chemistry, but I was told that chemistry was an improper subject for young ladies. I want to study the medical books Dr. Smith lent me, but I fall asleep, because I am too tired. Jacob and I are in love. We have so little time together. I need to be with him."

"I understand what you mean about the sampler. I like looking at the sampler you made, but clothes would seem to be more important. Studying medical books is not a proper use of a young lady's time."

"Dr. Smith told me that I was a big help to him. When we had to quarantine the guests with smallpox, I helped the doctor take care of them. Remember, you were visiting Mrs. Kinnen when Kara went into labor. Dr. Smith said he needed help, so I was there with her. It was so wonderful seeing her little boy born! How can learning about birthing be improper for a young lady?"

"The point is that you do need to take time to prepare for your life with Jacob."

"I need to be with Jacob. We aren't even allowed to kiss, because we don't have a private place to be together."

"Esther, we are only trying to protect your reputation. Some people are still telling bad things about the time you were attacked. We have to keep things proper with Jacob."

"I can guess who has been telling lies! I'll tell you something just to show you how wrong those gossips can be. Last year, I heard that the baby must be someone else's baby, because Ira could not father a child. I laughed when I heard it, and I told the gossip that the baby looks more like his namesake every day! Mama, I don't think this decision belongs to the gossips!"

Millie sat on her bed. "I know we need to have cool heads to think. Let's sleep on it. I'll talk to Ira and Kara. We will pray for a good decision."

"You won't tell them about the gossip, will you?"

"There is no need to hurt Kara. As you said, Baby Ira is the living image of his father."

"Ira is so proud of his son. I wouldn't like to see what might happen to the person that told him that lie."

"Neither would I," Millie agreed.

Esther lay in her bed, thinking, that night. *Mama wants me to wait a whole year! It's too much to bear. My Jacob might be gone forever. Ira is the one that will not let us have any time alone. He does take the time to chaperone us, though. Maybe he will want us to wait longer. What will happen tomorrow? Will Jacob get permission to marry me? Jacob and I may be able to convince Mama, but Ira is not swayed once he makes up his mind.*

Esther awoke in the morning to find her mother gone from the room. She washed in the water she brought to the room the night before. She rushed to dress and go to the outhouse. This was their Sunday off from work till after church. *Jacob might ride his horse to our church in the city, today. I hope so. I want to see him. At least I can sit near him. Although, when I see him, I don't want him to leave. It hurts me to know that he goes home to that gossip monger that spreads lies about me.*

Esther met her mother in the kitchen where they shared one large hot cake. Esther couldn't help but notice that her mother was very subdued. She said very little, as though she was very sad. *I wish my mama would not be sad. I love her, but I have to leave her so I can be with Jacob.*

Jacob was waiting for them at the door of the church. Millie looked at both of them and said, "After church, we will all go to the hotel. Ira and Kara will find a place for us to talk."

The rooms were full at the hotel, so Ira suggested they go to Millie and Esther's room. Jacob had never seen the room where Esther lived. He looked around the room, and then looked at Esther. He said nothing, but Esther decided that he might better understand her desire to have a space of her own.

Jacob sat on the chair, while everyone else sat on the beds. Kara held the baby in her arms till he wanted to get down and walk. Esther held her breath as Ira began to speak. "Dis is not da way dis is done, now. Jacob and Esther's father would go and talk. Esther's father cannot be here, so all of us will have to do dis t'ing. Young man, you have something to say, ya?"

Jacob cleared his throat and hesitated only a second before speaking. "I want to … I am asking for Esther's hand in marriage." Jacob took a deep breath, as though it had taken all his breath to say the short sentence.

Ira nodded, and asked, "Have I been hearing dat you will go to California, ya?"

"There is gold in California. I plan to go there and make my fortune."

As Esther looked at each face, she thought she saw tears forming in her mother's eyes. She forced herself to be quiet. She had hoped to talk about going to California another time.

Ira said, "I will tell a story, now, ya? I can tell ya want da answer before da story. Millie, you will hear dis first, now, ya? When da story is done, den you talk to da young ones in love."

"Kara and me were in da old country. We fell in love when we were children. At school, I would court her at recess. I was done wit' school. I started to think it was time to start courtin' her proper. I asked her fadder if I could call on her. I didn't know that her fadder and my fadder had a fight over a chicken, no less. Kara's fadder put me out of da house, faster'n a cricket can find a crack. Kara and me, we would sneak about to talk. We waited for da grown up people to get over their arguin'. Den Kara's fadder heard stories about Kara and me, wit our meetin in the bushes. Dat was not gud."

"Both of us, so crazy wit love, we planned a way. Kara's sister carried our notes we wrote. Kara told her mudder and fadder she had to go away. She could not bear to see me walkin' on da street when she was not to talk wit' me. She went to stay wit' her mother's sister by the sea."

"I told my mudder and fadder da same ting. I said I would be goin' across the sea to da new country. My mudder din wan dis, but she was seein' how sick I was. Fadder gave me money. I bought da passage for two wit da money. Da parents knew not a t'ing. Dey wouldn't talk to one anudder. Kara slipped out a' da house to me. Da preacher married us. He said he shouldn't wit'out any fadder givin' his blessing, but he did." Ira hesitated.

Kara said, "We had no babies for so long, I t'ot maybe, God was sayin' we did a bad t'ing. Now, here is little Ira."

Ira raised his voice. "It was a bad t'ing dat our fadders did. Millie, you see, now?

What kind of an answer we give to da young ones, ya?"

Millie's voice was hoarse when she began to speak. "Our parents were very upset when we told them we would go to America. We were married, so there was nothing they could do. I still can't say it was a mistake."

"Jacob," Millie said, "Everything in me wants tell you that you can't take my daughter to California, but I won't. You and Esther can be married, before you go to California."

Esther and Jacob hugged each other.

Kara poked Ira on the arm to get his attention when he started to leave. He quickly said, "Dare will be a proper weddin'. Esther will have all da friends and all dat. No small t'ing for this to do! All come here for da party."

Ira held the door for all to leave, except Esther and Jacob, and said, "Five minutes and the two of you are in da kitchen." The door closed. They listened to the footsteps as everyone left.

"Jacob," Esther said.

"You promised!" Jacob interrupted.

The two locked in a strong embrace and the passionate kiss that Esther had imagined.

"Esther!" Jacob said, "I don't want to wait, either. We have to plan the wedding. How soon can this be done?"

"Well, we have to talk to the preacher before we set a date. I need to get a dress ready. It's up to you to get the marriage license. We have to plan the journey to California."

"Let's talk later," Jacob said, "I want another kiss."

As they walked to the kitchen, Esther asked, "Have you told your mother that you would ask for my hand?"

"I'll have to tell her, now. I decided to wait till your mother gave her permission."

"What does your father say about us?"

"I told him I was asking, and he said my mother would be happy. I told him that she would not be happy with the bride I chose. He told me that he will tell my mother to be happy."

Esther laughed, "I don't think that will work. At least, **he** doesn't hate me."

"I don't think my mother **hates** you."

"She says awful things about me."

"She had better not say anything about you. I will tell her to watch what she says about my bride to be. What does she say?"

"I will tell you the next time we are alone," Esther said, as they reached the kitchen.

Kara looked up from her work, and said, "Esther, tomorrow you and Millie and me, we will go ta see Mrs. Kinnen. She can make the proper dress for you. That is what Ira says we'll do, now."

"Oooh! Thank you so much, Kara. I never thought I would have a dress made for me!"

"You are my only girl, ya know. I can't have you wed in any old t'ing."

Esther noticed a strange bewildered look on Darby's face, as he looked at Jacob, and at Kara.

The next time Esther was working with Darby, she talked on and on of the wedding plans. She could tell there was a question in Darby's mind, and so she decided to give him a chance to ask it.

Finally, at the end of the day, Darby asked, "In this country the two can be wed without a man's parents to be givin' the blessing, then?"

"The bride's parents seem to have the most to say about it here," Esther said, thoughtfully. "Jacob's father would give his approval for our wedding. It's a good thing we don't have to get his mother's approval. We wouldn't be getting married. My mother gave us her permission."

Darby had a broad smile on his face, but he said no more about it.

I suppose I won't ever find out what that was all about. I wish we could stay in touch with things here after we leave for California.

6

ROMANTIC GETAWAY

THE DAY OF THE WEDDING WAS SUNNY BUT cool, with softly blowing breezes. Esther woke to watch the light of dawn begin to light the room. Her dress was hanging in plain sight. Stuffing the dress into the chiffonier would have caused wrinkles in the voluminous skirt.

Mrs. Kinnen also gave her a skirt and blouse that was not as fashionable as it was sturdy. She called it a traveling dress. "This will be our little secret," Mrs. Kinnen said, as she showed Esther the panels on the inside of the skirt that allowed the skirt to split. "You can't ride side saddle all the way to California. This is my present to you, Esther," she said. When Esther thanked her, she said, "I thank **you**. You are as wonderful as your dear mother. You know how to take all the bad things and let them go by you without sticking." In a strange way, Esther knew what she meant.

By now, the whole community knew Esther would be traveling west with two men. *Today is not about going west. Today is the celebration of the two of us on our wedding day!*

Esther stood at the altar with Leah by her side. Jacob's brother, Alton, stood up with him. *Jacob looks frightened. He can hardly get the words out.*

Suddenly, it seemed, the two of them were married. They kissed in public, for all their friends and relatives to see.

Esther noticed that everyone was smiling at her and Jacob, except her new mother-in-law. She had a pained look on her face. *I will try to make peace between us. When we leave for California, she may never see us again. She should let go of her hateful feelings.* Esther held her husband's arm a bit more firmly as they walked past her down the aisle as man and wife.

When Jacob and his brother went to hitch up the buggy, Esther saw her chance to speak. Mrs. Durham was also standing alone, and Esther said, "I want you to know that I love your son very much. I plan to be a good wife for him."

Mrs. Durham did not smile. In fact her face was full of disdain as she said, "I want you to know something, young woman. A woman's reputation follows her, no matter how far she goes. You will accomplish nothing by taking my son so far away from me."

Esther reeled within from the power of the cruel words. When she regained some of her composure she said, "My reputation is better than you believe. I had nothing to do with Jacob's decision to go to California. The only question was whether to take me with him!"

Before Mrs. Durham could reply, Mrs. Kinnen approached. "Esther," she said, "I just wanted to tell you that I think your father would be so proud of you today. I can't help but think he's popping his shirt buttons with pride as he looks down from heaven."

"Why, thank you, Mrs. Kinnen. That was the one thing you could say to make this day happier." Esther could almost hear a *harrumph* coming from her new mother-in-law.

Mrs. Kinnen and Esther shared a knowing smile. Esther asked, "What can you tell me about my father? My mother just tells me he was a wonderful man."

"That part is true. He was so much in love with your mother, but he was good to all he met. He made us all laugh with his stories. When he got sick and died, everyone on the ship suffered the loss, along with Millie."

Esther smiled at Mrs. Kinnen as she moved toward the carriage Joshua drove. *I will hold my tongue. I will not tell Jacob how cruel his mother has been. He does not need to know. His mother is hurting, so she lashed out at me. I will not be fanning the flames of anger between us. I must forgive her. Someday I will forgive her, but for today I will not let her anger ruin my day.*

Esther could not believe the wonderful reception held in the hotel dining room. Kara had made a wedding cake. There was a long table full of food. Kara whispered to Esther, "When everyone heard about the reception for you, they said, 'We want to help.' I couldn't tell dem not to bring."

Ira made his way through the people toward Esther and Jacob. When he reached them, he said, "Come outside, ya?" He held the door open for both of them as they walked out. "Da wedding present is out here, now, you see dat, ya?"

Esther saw Harris Kinnen, and then she saw that he was holding the reigns to a pair of horses. "Horses! You are giving us horses?" Esther approached the mare. "She's beautiful!" The mare lifted her head with her ears perked forward as Esther petted her on the muzzle.

"Dey are **strong** horses," Ira said, proudly. "Mr. Durham found dem, and he paid half, so dis is from both of us. Horses dat can go all da long way ta California."

"Thank you both so much!" Esther said. "Horses are the perfect gift!" Esther stood on tiptoe and kissed Ira on the cheek, as Joshua shook his hand. Ira's eyes widened at the display of affection, but he smiled. Esther turned to Mr. Durham and thanked him, also.

Jacob said, "Thank you, sir," to Ira and his father. He walked around the horses, checking them with his hands. "They are very strong. They couldn't win a fast race, but they'll go the distance."

Esther looked at her new father-in-law to find him watching her and smiling. "You really do like the gift?" he asked.

"Of course I like them. They are exactly what we need."

Mr. Durham looked pleased.

Esther put her arm up to pat her horse's neck and said, "I'll name her Joy because she was given to me on a joyful day."

The next few nights were spent in the hotel room Ira provided for them, and the days were spent preparing for the trip.

One day Joshua took Esther to the shooting range, so she could practice with her pistol. Elliot joined them there. He was a thin man, an inch shorter than Jacob. He had a beard that was darker than his light hair. He said nothing as Esther shot as well with the pistol as he did with the rifle at close range.

"Do we have a wagon being built?" Esther asked.

"We don't plan to take a wagon," Elliot said. He watched, carefully for Esther's reaction. "We can take a straighter, shorter path if we are on horseback."

"We can't possibly carry all we need on our horses," Esther told him.

"We'll take a packhorse with a tent. The army does it that way when they are in a hurry. It's important that we get there quickly, so we get the best chance at a gold mine."

Esther could tell there was more on his mind. *He's hoping I'll say I won't go without a wagon. I won't give him that pleasure.* "You think we will make slower progress because I am coming, don't you?"

Elliot blushed at her question. After glancing at Jacob, he said, "Now that you asked, I think we might not get there if you come along. You will most definitely slow our progress."

"Jacob is going, so I am going too. I can't stay here and wonder what has become of him."

Elliot looked away from Esther's determined gaze.

Esther went back to concentrating on the pistol practice. The first bullet didn't even hit the target. *Calm yourself. You are so angry that you are shaking when you try to keep the gun on target.*

Elliot laughed. He took his turn next. He also missed the target with his rifle.

Jacob hit the target with his rifle. He carefully replaced the target they were using. When he came back to Esther, he said, "That's a difficult target for a pistol."

"I will hit it this time," Esther told him. Esther carefully leveled the pistol, but she was determined not to take too much extra time before firing. *I will show Elliot that I can shoot as good as any man!* She hit the target.

When the day came to leave, Joshua's parents came to the hotel to see them off. Millie, Kara and Ira were out on the sidewalk, also. Mrs. Durham said, "Goodbye, my son," as she kissed his cheek. She ignored Esther.

Millie could not hide her tears. "You come back to me if this trip proves too hard," she said. "Traveling on horseback is just too hard for a woman."

I am so tired of everyone thinking that a woman is less than a man. At least she didn't call me a girl. Finally, she realizes I'm a woman. "I promise, Mama. I'll miss you the most. I'll miss Kara and Ira and the baby and everyone. I promise to send a letter as soon as I can."

Leah walked up to Esther and said, "I couldn't stay at school when you are leaving," she said. "Actually, the teacher gave me permission to go when I told her you were leaving today."

Esther gave her a hug. Maybe someday there will be a train to California, so you can visit us."

"You dreamer! You always did believe in the impossible!" Leah said. "You wouldn't go after the gold if you weren't an impossible dreamer. That's not for me. I'll stay here and go to normal school."

"With so many people going west, someday you may be teaching in the west."

Esther saw Jacob's mother wince, and turn away.

"I know God is with us," Esther said to everyone. "Someday, all of you will know that."

Esther rode side saddle, so she could see everyone waving as they rode out of town. She swung her leg over when her mother was out of sight. *I feel so free! No more chamber pots. No more standing by the hot stove. I'll be in the fresh air! This trip will be hard, but I will show Elliot that I **will not** slow them down. They need me! Women are not a liability. I'll be with Jacob, so I'll be happy. I like to ride! Now I can ride all the way to California.*

Elliot was soon ahead of both of them, as he urged his horse on to the fastest walk without putting his horse into a trot.

"We have a long way to go," Jacob called out., "Pace the horse. Your horse knows a good pace. Let him go at his pace."

Reluctantly, Elliot did as he was asked.

7

HARD TRAVELING

THE THREE WERE CAMPING IN PENNSYLVANIA. THEY WERE surrounded by oak trees and bushes near the river. They had gathered enough dry, fallen wood to keep the fire going for the night.

Esther was washing out the cotton for her monthly flow. The rocks in the river were her washboard and a tree branch served as a clothesline. After Esther finished the washing, she gathered dry moss from the bank that faced north by the river.

"What are you doing, now? You don't need a soft bed of moss," Elliot grumbled.

Esther hesitated, as she did not want to explain. The moss was soft and absorbent. Leah had taught her to use it when they were riding. She had said, "My mother thinks I should stay home and be *indisposed,* but I use the moss inside my cotton pad, so nothing runs through."

"I need it between the saddle and my skin," Esther told him. *I hope he understands what I'm saying, so I don't have to tell him the exact purpose. I have so little privacy. At home, no one knew of my bodily functions except my mother.*

"Get some for me, too," Elliot told her.

Esther could not believe her ears. Then a thought occurred to her, so she asked, "Elliot, do you have saddle sores?"

Elliot blushed, but said nothing. Jacob looked at him, too, and said, "Esther knows about saddle sores. Answer her."

"Yes," was his reply, as his blush became a deeper shade of red.

"Elliot, you should have said something. We can treat it with salve."

"I took some of your salve, but it didn't help."

Esther remembered the pained look when Elliot dismounted, but she thought he was commenting on having to stop so soon for her womanly duties. "Elliot, this is serious. Dr. Smith would send some of his patients to the hotel to stay. One man died from an infection in his saddle sores."

"They hurt me bad, but I won't die."

"Jacob, look at his sores. Tell me if they are full of pus."

"I don't want a person lookin' at my saddle skin," Elliot insisted.

"Can **you** see it?" Esther asked. When Elliot did not reply, she said, "You know more of my business than I want you to know. Now you tell me you want to keep your saddle sores private? Let Jacob see those sores, and then go wash them in the stream. After that let them dry."

"Hell, then look at them yourself!" Elliot said angrily, as he turned, dropped his pants and bent over.

The sores were large, red and weepy. Esther did not see any sign of infection. "One thing you need is some soft cotton underwear. That heavy material in your pants is rubbing you raw."

"Why doesn't Jacob have sores?"

"Jacob has done more riding. His skin is toughened up. He also wears underwear. Your saddle might not be the right fit for you. Before these sores started, you should have gotten off your horse and walked, so your skin could toughen up."

"Then my feet will hurt," Elliot complained.

"Do you have blisters on your feet, too?" Jacob asked.

"Yes, don't you?"

"No, I went to a good boot maker for a good pair of boots when we first talked about the trip."

"I didn't have enough money for that," Elliot replied. "I bought a new saddle."

Jacob said, "That's another reason you have sores. A saddle has to be broken in to fit your body. You will have to stop riding till you heal."

Esther stood, smugly remembering the times Elliot accused her of slowing their progress. She bit her lip to keep herself from delivering a comment. She had a long way to go with this man. She knew that she would have to pay the cost of keeping the peace.

The tent was set up in case of unexpected rain, but the night felt warm, so they slept outside. As Esther lay awake that night, she could hear the soft breathing of her husband beside her and some soft snoring coming from Elliot, a few paces away. She had placed her pistol over her head, just inside the tent. Some of the women had warned her that she would attract wolves during this time. She didn't know if it was true, but the gun would be within reach. There were other vermin that would be attracted to their food.

My mother was right. I left her all alone. She must be so lonely. Traveling by horseback is too hard for me. I may not have open sores like Elliot, but I am sore all over. I wish I could talk to my mother. I wish I could talk to any woman. I can talk to

Jacob and he pretends to understand, but Elliot is right there. Elliot rolls his eyes and makes snide comments. I have to eat the meat we can shoot or snare. I am hungry most of the time. I am sick of the food cooked on an open fire. I want to cook on a stove. I didn't know how lucky I was to be able to get up and eat a fresh hot cake off the grill. Esther went to sleep dreaming of being back at the hotel. Some time later, Esther became aware of some sounds that didn't belong. Joy, her horse, made some soft noises. She heard other horses moving. Esther was so tired, she lay there hoping to go back to sleep. Suddenly, she heard her mother's voice say, "Esther, wake up!"

Esther lifted her head to see an outline of a man on a horse, leading another horse toward the path by the river. Joy was missing from the spot where she had been staked. Esther could hear Elliot continuing to snore. Jacob was beside her. *It's a thief! A dirty horse thief! He can't take Joy, she's mine! I can't go anywhere without her! I might not even get back home!*

Esther reached above her head to get the pistol. She hoped she could shoot accurately in the moonlight. She sat up, leveled the gun by the weight of it, and fired toward the man's shoulder.

For a moment there was no difference in the scene. Esther was about to shoot again when the man cried out, "I'm hit! God damn you, Max! You were supposed to shoot 'em if they went for their guns!"

Esther saw the man had let go of Joy, so she stood and turned toward the next voice. Jacob moved and she presumed Elliot would also awaken.

A second voice called out, "I couldn't see anyone move! Let's move in before they can reload!"

The voice came from the northwest and Elliot was sleeping northeast of them, so Esther stood next to the tent, where she believed her outline would not be seen. She fired toward the noise of movement.

"A-a-ah! God damn it! I'm shot! Where the hell is it coming from?!"

The first voice said, "Let's get out of here! I'm bleeding! I'm bleeding a lot!"

Esther heard, "It's just me, Elliot. Don't shoot me, too." He went for his gun in the tent.

Esther went to her horse. She found the tether as she hugged Joy's neck. She could see the other three horses in the clearing where they had been staked. Obviously, the thieves had tried to take the nearest horse first. "Dirty horse thieves," she said softly. "They can't have you. You're such a good horse."

Elliot and Jacob had rifles in their hands, but all was quiet after hearing the thieves ride off. Esther went to Jacob. "Oh, Jacob, I've shot two men!" She cried into his shoulder. Jacob held her with one arm, as he had his rifle in the other.

"Esther, you had to shoot," Jacob said. "They were going to kill us. Calm down. We have to move **now.** We can't wait for daylight. Those men may have friends or relatives who will look to get even. We have to find a town with some lawman, or at least put some distance between us and those thieves."

Esther needed to stand and calm herself as the men began to pack up. She had imagined a lot of uses for her gun, but she did not ever think she would shoot a white person. Her head knew Jacob was right, but she still had a nagging guilt.

Esther was only vaguely aware of what the men were doing. Jacob said, "We can't go back to that store we were in yesterday. One of those voices sounded familiar. I think he was one of the men by the store who was talking to us. . . Esther! Come on! We're almost ready to go! Get your horse!"

Esther went to get Joy even though she was still shaking. She could put the saddle on in the dark with no problem. They walked a short way till they found the path in the moonlight. They mounted and rode. Dawn was a welcome sight, but they kept moving. Silently, they rode till morning was a reality, and then the men began to tell their perception of what happened.

Jacob had repeated for the second time that the gunshot had awakened him, when he asked, "Esther, what woke you?"

Esther thought a moment. *I want to say that women tend to wake easier from noises. I won't tell them that. They wouldn't believe me, anyway. I can't tell them my mother woke me. They would think I was crazy.* "I heard Joy moving and the stranger's horse."

Elliot said, "Well, Jacob, it's a good thing you brought Esther to protect us men, or we would be walking to California."

Jacob chimed in, "I'm glad I brought her, too. Those horse thieves would have shot us if the lookout had seen us go for our guns."

Esther silently relished the moment. She knew that they would not have been able to go anywhere without horses. The trip to California would have stopped. They would be at the mercy of anyone they could find to help them get back home.

A little way down the road, Elliot said, "Esther, would you mind not telling the story of how you saved us?"

"Who am I going to tell? Any people we meet might be related to the horse thieves. I don't want to talk about it, anyway. I shot two men. They weren't dead when they left, but they will probably die of infection. They deserved it, but I'm still not proud of it." Esther hesitated, and said, "I promise not to tell the story for at least 10 day's travel."

When they finally dismounted to water the horses, Esther could see dark red spots on Elliot's pants. "Elliot, you're bleeding," she told him.

"I packed some of the moss you picked up. Would that help? It doesn't hurt as bad."

"It would stick to the wound. Take off your pants and cover yourself with my shawl," Esther suggested. "You should walk so the sores can dry."

"Somebody might see me."

"Elliot, she's right." Jacob said. "Those sores have to heal, or we will have to turn back."

Elliot muttered under his breath, and then said, "Where's your shawl?"

Esther handed the shawl to Elliot. She usually wore it around her hips, covering the gun and holster, but it was making her warm on that day, anyway. Esther turned her face away as Jacob helped Elliot secure the shawl about his waist. "You have to wash the blood out of your pants, now," Esther told him, as she pointed toward the river.

"I'll do it later, after we eat."

I can't believe this is the man that we're trusting to show us the best trail to California with his compass. He is so stupid about some things. Esther told him, "The blood won't wash out, even with lye soap, if it dries in. If you don't mind, I don't care."

I do care, but I won't tell him what he looks like with dark spots on the back of his pants. What a lot we are! I don't even have my hair combed.

Esther got out the campfire biscuits she'd saved from last night's supper. They even had a bit of butter, bought at the store. All of it would taste like the tin it was stored in, but she was hungry, so she would eat her share. Jacob took off his boots and waded to the middle of the river to get the clearest water in the canteens. Elliot had taken the lye soap, and was washing his pants, nearer the edge downstream.

Esther laid out the food from the tin, and then she looked for her comb and brush. Suddenly her heart sank as she remembered leaving them in the tent. "Jacob! Did you pack up my brush and comb when you packed the tent?"

Jacob thought a moment, and then said, "I didn't see it, so I don't know. Elliot, did you see it?"

"It was too dark under the trees. We couldn't see anything," Elliot called out.

Esther took the tent off the pack horse, and spread it out on a grassy area. Her brush and comb were gone. *My hair will be one big rat's nest by the time I get something to keep it straight. I'm ready to go home now! Maybe I can persuade Jacob that Elliot can't make the journey because of his saddle sores. I don't want to take the blame for the failure. Not after what Elliot said when we started. I'll bide my time awhile. There will be a time when Elliot will be ready to go home, too. My mother told me I could come back if it was too hard.*

"Do you want to camp here?" Elliot said, hopefully, when he and Jacob came up from the stream carrying their boots.

"That's a good idea," Jacob said. "We should let the horses graze awhile, anyway."

The three of them unpacked the horses before they ate the small meal. Esther pulled a piece of grass just below the forming seeds, exposing the tender end.

When Elliot saw her chewing on one end of the grass, he asked, "Are you so hungry you're ready to graze with the horses?"

Jacob pulled a piece for himself. "Try it," he told Elliot. "Just chew on the end. You'll be loose as a goose if you eat the whole thing."

Elliot pulled a piece. "It's sweet!" he said, after he tasted it.

I grew up in the city, but I learned more than this city boy.

For two days, all three walked most of the time. Esther would get on her horse when she tired of walking.

On the third day Elliot said, "There's smoke!"

They both looked the same way he was looking, to see a small stream of smoke moving above the trees. No one had to say anything. They knew that smoke during the day meant that somebody was cooking. "I hope it's a house," Esther said softly. *Country folk are so hospitable. We would leave the house with our stomachs full of good country fare.*

Each quickened their steps. When the house was visible, Elliot said, "I'm putting my pants on." He stopped and got on the far side of his horse to take off Esther's shawl. His pants had been hanging from his saddle horn. He handed the shawl back to Esther.

As they approached the log farmhouse, they saw sheep grazing. A dog came toward them, barking furiously. The horses moved about in fright, but did not run.

Esther saw a gun barrel come out the door. A female voice said, "Just get back on those horses and get outa here! There's a store down the road, ten miles. Take your business there."

"Ma'am, we're traveling to California. We mean you no harm," Jacob said.

"Take your meanin' me no harm down the road," the voice said.

"Ma'am, I would like to ask for the use of a comb," Esther said. "I lost mine."

The gun barrel lowered. A woman with brown hair done up in a bun stepped into the doorway. "Land sakes!" she said. "Why didn't you tell me there was a woman with you? Come on in!" She spoke to the dog, "Fritter! Stand guard."

"I'm Ina Stafford. I'm sorry about puttin' a gun on ya, but I have to take care."

"Believe me, I understand," Esther told her. "I'm Esther Car. . . . Excuse me! I mean Esther Durham, and this is my husband, Jacob, and his friend Elliot Rivers."

As she busied herself making food, Ina said, "Lost your comb, you say. You don't have lice, do ya? I don't need to be usin' my good kerosene to wash the lice out."

Esther barely had time to shake her head when Ina said, "Well, go to my bedroom and fix your hair. There's a piece of a mirror there. My own face is the only female I see between trips to the store." She talked fast, as though she was in a hurry to get the words out.

Esther combed her hair the best she could and pinned it back. As she walked back to the kitchen, she heard Ina tell Elliot, "Will ya have a chair? Yer makin' me nervous standin' there."

"He has saddle sores," Esther explained. Elliot gave her a pained look.

"I can fix you a chair you can sit on," the woman said with confidence. She left her stove to go into another room. She brought out a piece of wooly sheepskin and folded it so the weight would be off the sores. "Put your sittin' bones on that," she told him.

Elliot carefully sat on the chair. A look of surprise and delight came over his face.

The woman smiled, knowingly. "There's nothing like sheep's wool for comfortin' the saddle sores."

"Ma'am," Elliot said, "When I get some gold, I'm going to see that you get a share of it."

"Ya think that's good, wait'll we get done with supper. I'll fix you up so you can sit a saddle, again."

When supper was finished, Ina asked Elliot if he had an extra pair of pants. She took an awl and a needle to some scraps of tanned, wooly sheepskin, attaching them inside the pants. She covered the area of the legs and backside, where the skin would hit the saddle. "Go in the bedroom and put 'em on," Ina ordered. "Then I want you to go out and get into the saddle."

When Elliot got into the saddle, his eyes widened. "It's unbelievable!" he said. "Woman, if you weren't a married woman, I'd be proposin' right now! Your share of gold just got bigger."

"I **am** married, and don't even talk to me about gold. My shiftless husband promised me he'd settle down and stay home with me. He heard about the gold in California, and he was gone. Somebody has to stay with the sheep, so here I am. His family is right down the road, so they help out some, but most of it is up to me. The baby's a comin' in six months, so he'll have a child to come home to, if I ever see him again."

"You are doing well for your condition," Esther commented, as they walked back toward the house.

"I don't get sick like some women do. I just work. I had two babies, but lost them both to the fever. I hope I get to raise this one. There's nothin' worse than losin' a child. I thought I couldn't stand to have another one, but here it is, I'm havin' it, and my man is long gone."

Esther couldn't put in a word, as Ina kept talking at a speed she couldn't compete with.

"You boys may as well take those saddles off," Ina called out. "This woman needs to stay a night and sleep in a bed. If you won't have trouble catchin' 'em, put the horses in the pasture." When they were in the house, Ina looked at Esther's gun and asked, "You need **that,** with two men to look after you? Or do ya need it to keep the other one off ya?"

"I got this instead of an engagement ring. My husband won it in a shooting contest. It comes in handy on the trail."

"I'll bet it does," Ina said with one eyebrow raised. She was quiet for a few seconds, with a skeptical look on her face. "I can't hit anything with a pistol, myself. Don't tell anybody, but I don't do too good with a rifle, neither."

"My husband and I practiced together for the contest before we were married."

"I didn't even know my man. My folks and his got together and told us we were to be wed, that was it."

"Did you grow to love him?"

"What's to love? He stays around long enough to get a little one on the way and he leaves. Maybe if this one lives, he'll stay with me. Even his own folks just throw up their hands. Your man is made different. I can tell. He loves you."

At bedtime, Ina said, "You newlyweds take the big bed. I'll make a bed out here for the other man. I can sleep on the small bed for one night." She laid a large sheepskin blanket on the floor, and handed Elliot a cloth blanket as she said, "Git yer other pair of pants. They'll be fixed for ya in the mornin'. Put these under shorts on to keep the wool from stickin'in the sores. I made 'em for my man, but he up and left before I got 'em done."

Before they left in the morning, Jacob told Ina, "Take this money for the sheepskin."

"I'm takin' one piece of your money, so I can buy the goods I need for the tannin' of more sheepskin, that's it. You have a little lady there without a comb or a brush for her hair. Buy her what she needs at the store. It's about ten miles down the road. Don't let 'im put 'is prices too high. He'll do it if ya let 'im. If ya see Jack Stafford on yer way, anywhere, or in California, tell him he's got a baby coming. I wasn't so sure when 'e left."

They could hear Ina continuing to talk as they rode away. Esther thought she heard the phrase, "Poor fools!"

When they were down the road a mile, Jacob said, "I wonder if she's quit talking yet."

Elliot said, "I think I know why her husband left."

Esther couldn't help herself. She laughed aloud, but then she said, "He should still stay with her. She is a loving, giving woman. He could spend a lot of time in the barn, or something. It's a low thing to leave a woman when she's having your child. She wouldn't feel the need to talk so much if she had someone there to talk with all the time." *I have never met anyone so outspoken. She says whatever comes to her mind. She should meet Jacob's mother. His mother thinks I'm impertinent? She should meet that woman.*

8

COPING WITH LOSSES

THE STORE WAS A TWO STORY, GRAYING, LOG building with a veranda. The top floor had curtains on the windows. There were men standing about outside. They quit talking as the three rode up. Elliot volunteered to stay with the horses while Jacob and Esther went inside.

The grey haired, balding man behind the counter carefully looked them over as they approached. His round face was tipped downward to look over his spectacles.

The prices for the flour and other supplies were reasonable, but when Jacob asked about a hairbrush or a comb, the man said he would have to look. He came from the back room and said, "Yes, I found something."

The brush was crudely fashioned, and the comb was small, like the moustache combs Esther had seen.

Jacob asked the price.

The man said, "One dollar. . . . each."

Jacob looked at Esther.

The man said, "We have to ship these in from back east, so they come high. If your lady needs it, you'll have to pay the price."

Esther was unable to say anything, because she was afraid of what may come out of her mouth. She shook her head.

"The lady says she'll do without, at that price," Jacob told him. "Can't you come down a bit?"

"As I said, they are shipped in, so I have to pay the freight."

That beady eyed buzzard! He knows we are travelers, so we won't be back again. He doesn't have to be reasonable. I don't think that brush would last through two brushings. I've never seen a brush so poorly made. I don't want it.

Esther shook her head again.

Jacob said, "We'll just take what we have on the counter."

When she got outside, Esther was fighting back tears. *How dare that man try to take advantage of us like that? He's as bad as those horse thieves. I would go back and yell at him if that brush was any good. He wouldn't make his wife use a brush like that!*

"I'm sorry, Esther," Jacob said as they packed up their purchases. "We'll get you a comb, somehow."

Elliot asked, "Didn't they have any combs?"

Jacob said, "There was an overpriced brush and comb. They weren't much good, though."

Esther got on her horse. She decided to wait to speak her mind. The strangers were sitting around watching her every move. *The last time there were men standing around, they were looking at what they could steal. Working men don't have time to stand around a store.*

When they were down the road, Esther told Jacob and Elliot what she thought. They listened to her without comment, till she stopped speaking.

Elliot said, "Maybe I should go back and tell him what you do to robbers."

"That was low, Elliot. If I can't tell that story, neither can you," Esther said angrily.

"You know that Elliot was only joking," Jacob said.

"I know, but I still think he shouldn't bring it up."

Neither one of them understands why the brush and comb is so important to me. It is part of what makes me human. I feel worse than an animal when I can't even comb my hair.

I have to remember, too, that I am no longer at the hotel where I have to be quiet and polite. I plan to forget about Jacob's mother and her opinion of me. I have a right to tell people when they offend me. Keeping the peace is one thing, but I will not keep all my feelings to myself.

That night Esther lay awake, thinking of all the miles they had ahead of them. *Why did I decide to go to California? My mother's words keep nagging at me. She must be so lonely. I would clean chamber pots all day for a chance to sit in the kitchen with my mother and eat one of Kara's pastries. Why did Jacob bring me here, on this God forsaken trip? God give me strength. I need it. How can I tell Jacob I want to turn back?*

Jacob stirred in his sleep. As Esther felt his warmth, she felt a small pang of guilt for blaming Jacob. *I was the one that said God would be with us.*

Esther was not aware of falling asleep, when she saw her mother standing beside her. Her mother's face looked so young and beautiful. Her mother spoke. "The home you long for is no longer there. You were right to go west with your husband. Keep going west till you find your home. Don't worry about me. I am happy here."

Esther was ready to get up and ask her mother how she found them when her mother disappeared. She looked about the campsite. She couldn't see anyone. Actually she couldn't see anything but shadows in the camp. The campfire had been put out to prevent a sudden wind from starting a fire. *How could I see my mother? It's dark here. She seemed to have an inner light. Maybe God is sending me a message. Why would God use the voice of my mother? I must have been dreaming. It was so real, but I must have been dreaming.*

Esther finally fell asleep. When she woke, Jacob was chopping wood. He picked up a piece of dry oak and began to smooth it with his knife. He worked on the wood while Esther made some breakfast. He put the wood away when they were ready to mount. *He's trying to make me a comb. He does understand! No matter what that comb looks like, when he's done it will be the most beautiful comb I've ever seen. Should I tell them about seeing my mother in a dream? Elliot would say I'm losing my mind. Maybe sometime I can tell Jacob. For now, I'll just keep going as long as God gives me strength.*

Esther was quiet that day. She went over her mother's words in her mind. She thought it was like a message from God. *Why would God use my mother's voice? It was a voice I should listen to.*

By the time the comb was finished, Esther's hair was a tangled mess. "Jacob, will you help me with the mess in the back? Esther asked. He came over and took the comb from her. "Start at the ends and work up," she told him.

After working on it for a few minutes, Jacob said, "I think we'll have to cut some of this out."

"No! We can't cut it! I won't even look like a woman! It will take years to grow out! If only we had some oil to put on it. That would help."

"The only oil we have is gun oil," Elliot said.

Esther turned to look at Jacob, "We'll have to use some of that. I can wash it out, later, but it will help with the tangles."

Minutes later, Esther's hair was a greasy mess, but the tangles were gone. It was a chilly morning, but she went to the river and washed her hair with lye soap.

Esther mounted with her hair hanging loose, so it could dry. As soon as her hair was dry, Esther put it up into a bun as she rode. She wore her bonnet to protect her face from the wind and the sun.

The three of them continued to ride west. *We would be going faster with a wagon. Elliot could lay down in the wagon when his saddle sores flare up, if we had a wagon.*

One day Elliot was talking of the home where he had grown up. "We had everything we needed," he said, "but nothing extra. I miss my mother's apple pie. She made the best pie for holidays, like Thanksgiving and Christmas. If we find gold, I will give my mother money so she won't have to sell most of the apples."

Jacob said, "I won't say I miss doing chores, like milking the cows with my brothers, but we had good times. I miss the talks we had, working together."

Esther was very quiet. Her list was too long to tell in a short time. *I miss my mother. I don't want to say that I miss the outhouse. I miss privacy. I miss all the little things I had at home when I thought I had so little. I could have found room for a needle and thread, but I didn't bring them. I miss Kara and Ira, and I miss being around people. I have always had a lot of people around. It's nice to get away from people for awhile, but I have no one to talk with except the people that have been with me. I have no one to tell about my day. If I had a journal, I could write in it, but we didn't bring a pen and ink. It would be hard to keep the paper dry.*

Jacob was asking, "Esther, what do you miss the most?"

Esther sighed, "Of course I miss my mother most of all." After a pause, she said, "I miss music. I can pray all day long, but I miss singing the hymns in church. I miss hearing music. On Saturday, we would have musicians come to the hotel to play happy tunes."

"I haven't heard a tune since our wedding," Jacob said, "I miss music, too."

"Maybe someone in California will have a musical instrument with them," Elliot said. "I miss hearing music, too." He hurried his horse for the first time in weeks.

9

DISHLAND

WEEKS OF TRAVELING HAD WORN OUT ESTHER'S RESOLVE to continue, but they had gone too far to turn back. Esther learned in conversation that the army did, indeed, travel shorter distances on horseback. They also had loaded wagons to back them up with supplies. Esther wondered how she would set up housekeeping in California. They only had a few meager supplies.

They followed a trail near a river for most of their travels, but now Elliot was convinced they could save time by making a straight path. Taking the advice of some strangers at a trading post, they left the trail in sight of the river. They bought a small barrel to carry extra water, packed some firewood, and set off across the plains.

The hard trip just got harder. The water was warm and tasted bad. They could see game, but it was often too far away to shoot. Esther had to be sure of her target if a rabbit jumped up close, because she had very little ammunition for her pistol. Still she kept the gun at her side for an emergency. Each day and each night, Esther prayed for strength.

The horses were allowed to graze in the morning till the dew went off the grass. They packed up and rode, slowly, in the heat of the day.

My brains are going to bake. I am so hot and tired. There is nothing but grass and sky. It seems we have been riding forever without seeing a real tree. The wind helps with the heat, but I wish I could have some rest from it. I hope Elliot didn't make a mistake with his compass. We should be coming to a river, soon. The deep grass is hard to ride through. I am getting seasick watching the grass wave in the wind.

Even Elliot is not asking us to speed up. I wonder if he has saddle sores again. His saddle sores have slowed our progress more than I have. I am so tired of riding. Standing by the cook stove doesn't seem so bad now. I was hot, but cool, fresh water was just outside. There was even a little ice to be had.

All were riding with their heads down. Not a word passed between them. Esther didn't want to open her dry mouth and expose it to the wind.

Suddenly, an unusual sight came into view. Esther was riding just ahead of the men. She reined in her horse to take in the scene. There was a perfectly round valley in the ground that resembled a giant serving dish. On the far side there was a scraggly little bush. As Esther moved her gaze downward, she saw the cabin. Down in the bowl, a short way from the bottom, there was a log cabin.

People! Water, cool water, for us and our horses! Maybe even a meal, or a place to stay inside for the night! We have to approach slowly, though. We have learned we are scary to some people. Oh, how I hope they are friendly. Maybe there will be a woman to visit with!

Esther urged her horse to move down the slope toward the cabin. Jacob and Elliot rode beside her, still without a word. Esther knew they were all thinking about the same things.

They had to ride by the cabin to the west side to find the doorway. The structure loomed larger than expected, as they stood on the ground. It had glass windows.

No one stirred. Esther was not frightened, but she had an uncomfortable feeling that something was wrong.

Jacob called out, "Is anyone home?" as he knocked on the door. There was no response, so he knocked again, harder. This time a small weak voice could be heard. Elliot stayed outside pumping water for him and the horses, while Jacob and Esther opened the door and walked inside. There was an entry way that looked like it may have been used as a small sitting room. As Esther's eyes became accustomed to the darker room, she saw a Bible lying on the small reading table. A decorative doily could be seen peeking out from under the Bible. The straight chair was sitting empty on the other side of the table. There was a colorful wall hanging, probably made by an Indian. *This cabin is a strange mixture of Indian and white people's things.*

Jacob led the way into the great room. On the far side of the room, Esther saw a cook stove. It was smaller than the one at the hotel, but larger than any she had seen in a private home.

The small weak voice came from a high bed to their left. In among the Indian blankets was a small Indian woman with blisters around her mouth. There were fewer blisters on her face and arms. A very small face of an infant could be seen on her left arm. The baby looked like a little Indian baby doll, as it did not stir.

Smallpox! This woman has smallpox! "It's smallpox," Esther said aloud to Jacob. Jacob went out the door to warn Elliot.

Esther approached the woman's bed. "Hello," she said.

The woman could hardly speak. Esther got closer to hear. "My angel," the woman said. "You are my angel. People come now?"

Esther went to the water bucket to get water, but the woman brushed the offered tin cup aside.

"I die, now," she said. When she saw Jacob, she looked back at Esther and said, "You my people the angel send. You be mother for Thomas." The woman took in a deeper breath. "Thomas, come!" She looked as if it took all her energy to call out. She rested a moment as she looked about.

Esther felt a gentle touch beside her. A little Indian boy with frightened eyes stood beside her, trying to get to the woman on the high bed. Esther got a chair for the boy to stand on. He stood on it and put his face where the woman could see it. When she saw him, she spoke again. "Thomas, this is mother for you." She looked at Jacob, and lifted her free hand to point at him, "This is father for you. God send them for you. Do what they tell you."

The woman closed her eyes a moment. When she opened them, she said, "Food for Thomas. You eat. Food good." She pointed, again with her free arm, over her head, toward the cook stove.

Esther walked over to the cook stove. She found a warm pot of vegetable stew there. There was meat in it, but she wasn't sure what it was. She put some of the small wood into the fire to get it going again. She wanted the stew to be hot. *That woman made food for her son with her last bit of energy!*

Esther went back to the bed and told the woman. "I found the stew. It does look good. We'll give some to Thomas as soon as it is heated. Where is Thomas' father?"

The woman had so much trouble speaking, Esther was almost sorry to have asked the question.

She smiled, ever so slightly, with her blistered lips. "He go east for gold pieces. He come home sick. Oldest son run to him. Hiram go, too late. We got sickness. Husband gone. He die someplace. He no come back. Caleb die from sickness."

"What is your name?"

"Summer. . . . . Names in Bible." The woman closed her eyes in exhaustion.

Jacob asked, "Did you understand all that?"

"Most of it," Esther told him. "Her husband went east to get some money, and he brought smallpox back with him. The oldest son ran to him when he saw him, so he got sick first. Her name is Summer. We'll find names in the Bible. She says God sent us here to take care of Thomas."

Esther saw the woman relax when she finished repeating the words. Esther could hear someone pumping water outside. *Elliot must still be watering the horses.* "Jacob, would you get me some fresh water, too?"

Jacob looked at the water pail and said, "That sounds good."

I can tell he's upset. He hasn't seen smallpox. I helped care for those people that broke out after they checked in at the hotel. Summer will probably die. It's a good thing we are both vaccinated. I don't think Elliot was vaccinated.

When the soup was hot, Esther put some in a bowl to cool for Thomas. Thomas had a few drying blisters around his mouth. She heated the tin bowl for Elliot's portion. Dr. Smith had told her that heat would keep smallpox from spreading. Elliot refused to come inside, so Jacob walked out to the doorway and handed Elliot the bowl of stew. Jacob, Thomas and Esther sat down to eat together. The table was just a plain pine table made from split logs, but it was elegant in Esther's eyes.

The stew tastes so good. I haven't eaten anything like this for so long. Elliot is all alone out there. Maybe we should eat with him, but I like eating inside.

Summer was stirring when they finished, so Esther mashed up a bit of stew for her. Again, she pushed it away. *I think the tiny baby is already dead. She is holding on to it, so we'll have to leave it there. We can bury them together when the mother dies. I shouldn't think like that, but Summer knows she will die.*

Esther looked about the home. There were two bedrooms. There was one larger room with a log double bed, and a narrower room with two small log beds. The blankets looked like Indian blankets. She pulled back the blankets on the large bed and found cotton sheets. Thomas watched her, carefully, but kept his distance.

"Jacob, we can sleep in a bed, tonight," Esther said, hopefully. She wondered if Jacob would sleep inside with the dying woman in the next room.

"Do you really want to sleep in here?" he asked.

"I really do. I am so tired of sleeping on the ground where I don't know what kind of creature will crawl in with me."

Jacob looked at the bed behind the curtained doorway. "Okay, I'll move our things inside, and help Elliot set up the tent."

Esther washed the dishes with hot water from the stove's reservoir. Esther smiled as she wiped them and put them away into the cupboard. *That is so nice. Just putting the dishes into their place in the cupboard feels wonderful. There's some fancy little china pieces here, too.*

As it got dark, Thomas went to his bed without anyone telling him to go. He was sleeping soundly when Esther peeked into his room. She lit a lamp from the fire in the stove and went into the large bedroom. *I wish I had a nightgown. I have slept in my clothes for so long.*

Jacob and Esther cuddled close and discussed the events of the day. Esther was happy to be talking to her husband with Elliot out of earshot.

In the morning, Esther went to check on Summer. She was breathing, but she didn't answer when Esther talked to her. Esther went to the outhouse. *Ah! Privacy! There are no bushes to hide behind on the prairie. Summer's husband must have loved her very much. He built this nice place for her.*

Thomas went outside while Esther put wood in the cook stove and made hot cakes. She found all the ingredients she needed in the kitchen. The milk was sour, but some baking soda sweetened it to make good pancakes.

Thomas came in when he was called. When he saw the hotcakes, he went to the area between the table and the water bucket and picked up the rug. His little hands picked up a metal ring in the floor and looked toward Jacob as he tried to lift a trap door.

"Oh!" Jacob said, "A root cellar." Jacob took the hint and opened the trap door. A lantern hung on the ladder descending to the cool storage area. Jacob lit a small sliver of firewood in the fire and lit the lantern. Together, Jacob and Thomas brought up a crockery jar. "We have jam for our hot cakes!" Jacob said.

"Unbelievable!" Esther said. "They must have found berries somewhere." Esther wiped the mold off the edge of the crock before using the jam.

Esther fixed a plate for Elliot and Jacob took it out to him. Then Jacob returned to eat inside with Esther and Thomas. As Esther started the dishes, Jacob came and asked her to step outside.

When she got outside, Jacob took a deep breath before he said, "We think somebody should find a town or a settlement, to see if anyone knows anything about any relatives. Elliot said he saw smoke to the north of here."

"The little boy still has blisters. We can't take him to town. For some reason he isn't as sick as the others, but he is still sick," Esther told him.

Elliot sighed.

Jacob said, "I don't know what to do. I don't want to leave you alone here, but I want to go to town with Elliot to check things out."

"I'll be alright here," Esther insisted. "I have a few bullets in the pistol if there's trouble. Someone should stay with Thomas. From what Summer said, there is no one that will be angry that I'm here. Look in the Bible at the names."

Jacob followed her back inside and he sat at the table in the great room as he looked at the names. Thomas walked over, sat in the chair beside Jacob and looked at him, expectantly.

Esther smiled and said, "Jacob, I think he wants you to read to him."

"Well, young man, we'll have reading time, later," Jacob told him. "Esther, Summer's full name is, *One Who Sings in Summer.*" Jacob read on. "The husband's name was Hiram Martinson, and a son named Caleb was born in 1843. Thomas was born in 1845." Jacob closed the Bible, got up and walked over to Esther. Thomas picked up the Bible and put it back in the small reading area.

"Esther, are you sure you'll be all right by yourself, here?"

"I'm very sure. I feel safe here. If you don't find anyone, you'll start back so you're here before dark, won't you?"

"Yes, and if there's a town, we'll pick up a few things and see what we can find out."

"I need a dress length, if we can afford it. I have the skirt that Mrs. Kinnen made for me, but my other dresses are in tatters."

Jacob kissed her on the cheek and hurried out the door. "I promise. We'll be back before dark!"

Esther listened to the horses leave and then she listened to the silence. There was a faint whisper of wind over the edge of the dish that reminded her of the sound of the ocean.

Esther checked on Summer. She was not breathing. Tears streamed down Esther's cheeks as she gently picked up Summer's hand. "Good-bye, beautiful lady," Esther said. *I knew her for a short time, but somehow she has woven her way into my heart. I wonder if there's a church in the settlement to the north. Obviously, this woman was a Christian. Maybe she has white friends. Maybe that's not possible. The men will help me bury her. I should look for Caleb's grave, so she can be near her son. It could be that he's by a church, but his white father wasn't here to bury him, so maybe not.*

Thomas watched as Esther cried. He came and hung onto her skirt. His eyes had no tears, but Esther could see sadness and fear.

Esther put on her tattered dress, so she could launder her one good skirt and blouse. She took the washtub off the side of the cabin outside, and she found lye soap. The washboard was hanging on the wall. She left her gun and holster on the bed.

Esther found clotheslines and hung the wash to dry. She had just come into the house when she heard horses. *The men are back, already!* Esther looked to the north as she ran out of the cabin. She saw nothing but grass, and then she realized that the sound was coming from the southwest. When she looked that way, she saw three Indians on horseback. She could feel a tug at her skirt as Thomas hid everything but his eyes.

They look peaceful. They have no weapons. At least I don't see any weapons. My gun is on the bed, so I hope I'm right. Thomas is part Indian, so they shouldn't mean to harm us.

There was one Indian with two feathers in a head band. One feather stood straight up from the middle of his forehead. The other feather hung down beside his ear. He rode a beautiful brown and white spotted horse. He was slightly ahead of the others. A round shield with a painted figure of an Indian man hung on the front his horse's breast near the left foreleg. The two younger Indians flanked the leader. They rode brown horses with black manes. They had no feathers.

The leader stopped his horse and said, "We come for Summer."

Esther took a deep breath, and said, "I'm sorry, but Summer died this morning." She held her breath, waiting for a reaction.

The men did not move and did not speak.

Esther noticed the travois behind the lead horse. *They know! I don't know how they know, but they know! Will they help me? No, they aren't moving! They expect me to carry her out. I have done a lot of things, but this. . . . . this is new thing I have to do.*

Esther said, "Wait a minute." She turned and went into the cabin. Thomas followed her. *I don't even know if they understood me when I told them to wait. They had better be there when I get outside. I hope I can carry her.*

Esther lifted the slight woman and the blanket under her from the bed. The baby slipped back onto the bed. Summer was lighter than Esther believed she would be. Esther carried Summer outside to find the Indian man had moved the travois so it was more accessible, but not much closer. She placed the dead woman on the travois as gently as possible. "Wait for the baby," Esther told them. She ran back into the house, fearing they would leave. She easily picked up the wrapped baby. She placed the baby in its mother's arms. There were leather thongs on the travois that Esther used to tie the woman and her baby in place together, so they would not fall out. As soon as Esther stepped away from the travois, the men left.

"Don't touch her!" Esther called out. "You might get the sickness if you touch her!" *I wonder if they understood me. The whole tribe will get sick if one of them gets smallpox. Now I'm worrying about Indians getting smallpox! I can't believe that!*

Thomas was at her skirts, again. *I wonder if he can talk. He has lost both of his parents and his older brother. His throat is probably raw from the smallpox lesions. We'll have to give him time.* Esther put her hand on the little boy's shoulder as they both watched his mother's body taken away. When there was nothing more to see, they stood a few more moments.

God, help me! I am here with this little half Indian and half white boy at my skirts. Now what do I do?!

10

THE DECISION

ESTHER WENT BACK INSIDE TO CLEAN SUMMER'S BED. She had cleaned similar beds at the hotel with her mother. Sudden death and death from smallpox had happened there. The hotel room had to be cleaned and aired to be ready for new guests. Esther took the blankets out to rinse them in the cold pump water. Under it all was a buffalo robe. She put that out on the dry grass in the sun to air. Esther realized that the high bed was the top half of a trundle bed in the narrower room. She was able to move it there. *Summer is gone, but I will not forget her.*

How can I convince Jacob to stay here? I want this home. Everything we need is here. Thomas is still sick. By the time he is well, it will be too late to go over the mountains to California this year. This is Thomas' home. He has lost so much. Does he need to lose his home, too? We have to stay here till spring, at least.

Summer's people must live near here. How did they know Summer was dead?

When the sun was lower in the sky, Esther went for a walk. Joy followed her, as though she missed being close to her. There was a wooden fence, north of the clothesline. *A garden!* Esther went back to the cabin to get a container and tools for gathering. She opened the gate and went into the garden. *We'll have new potatoes for supper. There is a lot of food here. We won't be hungry tonight, even if Jacob doesn't shoot a rabbit. This must be good ground for growing things. These are the biggest potatoes I have ever seen.*

Thomas followed wordlessly as she worked. He picked up the potatoes for her as she dug, and helped her pick some roasting ears of corn. Together, they carried the generous bounty to the cabin. Esther peeled the corn outside and gave the husks to Joy. She watched as Joy relished the treat. *That's why the fence is made so strong. Joy would help herself to the corn if the fence didn't keep her out.*

When the food was ready for the stove, Esther went outside to look for the men. She saw the horses coming over the edge of the dish. The pack horse looked as though it was loaded with something. *They must have found a town! I had better start cooking! They'll be here soon! I can't wait to tell Jacob and Elliot what happened while they were gone. I have never had a new story to tell them until now.*

Esther met the men at the doorway. As Jacob dismounted, he began talking. "Esther, you won't believe what happened! We found a road at the top of the rise. We followed the road till could see a town, but some men blocked our way. They asked where we came from and when we told them, they said we were not welcome in town. They said we would be shot if we went to town. We told them that we needed some supplies. They said that we would not live very long, so they would bring us some supplies out. They asked what we needed, and one man left.

We were under guard, there, till the man came back. We asked about the man that lived here. They said the man was a former sailor from the east. His father disowned him when he married an Indian woman. He lives east of here, but they didn't know where. Mr. Martinson came back from a trip and stopped at a neighbor's house. They all got sick and died. I tried to tell them that Elliot didn't go into the cabin, but that made no difference. I explained that you and I would not get sick, but they didn't believe me. When the man got back, he had a lot of food and supplies in a wagon. He put the supplies on the ground and backed off. He told us that when he told everyone about us, they gave us supplies. They wouldn't take any money for the supplies. They said the Johnson family got the sickness from a gold piece the sailor gave them. They took our names and the address of our families. They said they would notify our families when we died. They told us again that we would be shot if we try to go into town."

"Did they notify Mr. Martinson that his son has died?" Esther asked.

"They don't know where he lives, but they said he already thinks of his son as dead." Elliot told her.

"That is so sad," Esther said. "He will miss out on so much love because of his hate." Thomas had hid behind her skirts till he saw Jacob, and then he stood free and listened.

"I have a story to tell, too, but it can wait till after supper, now. I found some vegetables in the garden."

"We have fresh beef steak," Jacob said. Elliot carefully handed her a small package, standing as far away as possible. "Those people are generous. They don't even know us, but they gave us all this food."

"They don't want us sneaking into town, or going to any other family in the country," Elliot said.

"Whatever the reason, I'll cook this steak for supper tonight," Esther said. "We haven't had beef since our wedding day."

Esther saw Jacob look toward the empty space where the bed had been. "After supper," she reminded him.

Elliot's eyes grew wide when Esther brought out a plate of food. "There's butter here for the corn, too," Elliot said excitedly.

"We have more corn and potatoes if you want them," Esther told him.

After supper, both of them joined Elliot outside. In the twilight, Esther could see their eyes widen as she told of the Indians coming for Summer.

"What do we do now?" Esther asked when she finished her story.

The men looked at each other, and then back at Esther.

"We can't leave Thomas, and we can't take him with us," Esther said quickly.

"What do you want, Esther?" Jacob asked.

Esther noticed that Elliot was holding his breath as he awaited her answer. "I want to stay here," she said. "If we still want to go to California next spring, we can go then. There is shelter here from the cold of winter."

Elliot let out a big breath when Esther finished her first line and he spoke as soon as she finished. "I knew it," he said disgustedly. "I knew we shouldn't bring a woman along."

"It has been more than ten days travel," Esther told him.

Elliot stared at her a moment as if he didn't understand, and then a look of realization came over his face. "I'm sorry. We wouldn't have horses if you weren't along. No one could have foreseen this situation. We would not be this far west without you." Elliot turned his gaze, wistfully, to the west.

It was getting darker, so Esther didn't think the men could see her smile of satisfaction.

Jacob said, "It's settled, then. Esther and I will stay here to care for the boy. Elliot, we will divide up the supplies in the morning."

"You are going alone, Elliot?" Esther asked, incredulously.

"I heard talk of a wagon train just ahead of us. They're going west. Maybe they will let a man join them if I can catch them."

The next day, Jacob gave Elliot most of their pooled money and as much of the dry supplies as he could carry. They watched as Elliot rode straight west, leading the pack horse.

Did Jacob have to give him the big share of the money? Elliot has the money and supplies we would need to travel. I may never have to travel again. I can't believe he went on alone, but he might get smallpox if he stayed. God protect him. And God help us. The townspeople are afraid of us. Does this place have a name? I'll call this place Dish Land. My home is in Dish Land. Maybe this is the home my mother talked about.

11

NEW BEGINNINGS

ON THE NEXT RAINY DAY ESTHER WAS CLEANING and sorting. As she remembered the cold rainy days she had sat in the cramped little tent, she was grateful for the space to clean. Most of Summer's clothing was too short for her. Her own clothing was so ragged that she wore whatever she could find. *It's a good thing there will be no visitors. I will save my traveling skirt and blouse for when we are able to go to town. Mr. Martinson's undershirt will have to do for a blouse. Here's a new leather skirt that's too short, but I'll have to use it.*

Where should I put the cotton for my monthly? I should need it soon. No, it's past time to use it. That's why I feel sick before I eat in the morning! That's why I thought I was feeling seasick when I was riding on the plains. I'm not as bad as Kara was, but I have a bad stomach. I have to tell Jacob!

Esther went into the great room where Jacob was cleaning and oiling his rifle. "Jacob, I think we're going to have a baby!" she exclaimed.

Jacob continued to clean his rifle. "I thought so," he said in a matter of fact tone. "That's one reason we stayed here."

"You knew?"

"I wasn't sure, but I thought so."

He could have been a little bit surprised. I can't keep any secrets. I'll need to get a lot of things from town before winter. I need to make baby clothes. I'll need a dress that has a little extra room. I wonder how long we have to wait before we go to town.

The days were becoming shorter and cooler. On a warm afternoon, Jacob agreed to help Esther clean the ashes out of the cook stove. They put the hot coals into the ash can and made a fire in the small heating stove while cleaning. She pulled out the ash box below the fire box as she had done several times with the fire going. Jacob took that outside. She took the top of the stove apart and scraped the soot from there. She knew not to sweep all the ash off from under the top, as the oven heat would be uneven and her baking would be burned on top. She scraped the rest of the ash out from under the fire box into the ash bucket.

"Have you got it all?" Jacob asked as he was about to take hold of the ash bucket.

"I think so," Esther said in a tone that meant she was quite sure.

"Did you do this part?" Jacob asked; as he flipped open a door to a slot under the oven.

"Oh, I didn't know about that part," Esther said. "The yard boys always did this job at the hotel."

Esther put the little ash scraper into the slot to drag out the ash. As she pulled the tool forward, something solid dropped into the ash bucket. Esther looked into the bucket to see something round in it. Since her hands were already full of ash, she reached into the bucket and picked it up. As she brushed off the ash, the piece shone. "Jacob, it's gold! Look, it's a gold piece!" Esther put the tool in again. This time there were three gold pieces.

Jacob came over and took the pieces Esther offered him. His eyes widened. "Holy buckets!" he said, as he saw the gold for himself. "We'll have to strain the ashes before we make soap."

"Make soap? I don't know how to make soap," Esther said as she pulled more gold pieces out.

"I'll have to help you," Jacob said. "But if you keep bringing more gold out of that gold mine there, we can use store bought soap."

"Summer must have hidden it there. She put it in a place where someone who stayed here to care for Thomas would find it," Esther said as much to herself as to Jacob.

Thomas was watching, carefully. "Father bring gold," he said in a slightly hoarse voice.

"Thomas! You talked to us!" Esther said. "Does your throat feel better?"

Thomas nodded. "Father brought the gold," he repeated in a clearer tone.

"Well, Thomas," Jacob said, "This gold now belongs to all of us. We'll use it to build up this place with stock. We'll all make a good home here."

Thomas looked at both of them, wide eyed. Jacob continued, "What do you think, Thomas? Was your father planning for horses on this land, or cattle?"

"He said that we'll have more beef cows," Thomas said.

Jacob looked at Esther with surprise at Thomas' clear English. "Well, Thomas, we'll look for the best beef cattle we can find."

"He wanted to buy breeding stock from the Johnsons," Thomas said. "You said they are dead."

"Well, we'll find out what happened to the stock the Johnson's had," Jacob told him.

When Thomas decided to speak, he spoke. I wonder what else we said that he was taking into his little brain. He learned to talk from his father. He probably knows some Indian words, too. I was beginning to think he might be slow-witted.

For the next few days it rained. When it had been a month since they came to Dish Land, Jacob said, "Put on your best clothes, Esther. We're going to town."

"Is it safe? We don't want to be shot."

"They haven't seen you, and I'll shave my beard. By the time they figure out who we are, we'll have your dress material and such."

Esther looked at Thomas. His sores were just little pock marks on his face. "I want some yeast, too," she said. I'm so hungry for some raised bread."

"Your biscuits are good, but I would like some bread, too."

Esther shook her head as she looked at her faded bonnet, but she put it on. Her shoes were worn, also. "Jacob, how much of that gold are we going to spend?"

"None of it," he replied. "Today we'll spend what's left of our money. We know we'll have the gold when we need it later. Folks in town are afraid of those gold pieces."

"Does that mean I can have new shoes?"

"Yes, if we can find some," Jacob said. "There may not be much for women there."

I hope I don't have to wear men's clothes. I would like to dress like a woman.

"We need a wagon," Jacob said as they rode into town. "We need to get firewood before the snow comes. There are a few trees down by the river, but that's it. We need to get wood or burn some peat. Wood is easier to burn."

"What's peat?" Esther asked.

"It's some stuff folks get out of the bog that burns when it gets dry."

"I thought I knew about everything."

"Are you saying the city girl is dumb?" Jacob teased.

"I know a lot of things. I just don't know about that. We only used wood at the hotel."

"It's something folks use on the prairie. I don't know much about it either," Jacob admitted.

Suddenly Esther realized that Jacob had mentioned a river. "Jacob, where is the river? You didn't tell me you found the river."

"I went for a ride one day. The river is both south and west."

A little shiver of realization went down Esther's spine. *If we had ridden on a slightly different path we would have found the river, and we would have been traveling to California now. We would have missed Dish Land. The cabin can't be seen from miles away like the others on the prairie. That little boy getting on the horse behind Jacob probably would have died. Would the Indians have taken care of him? God, you must have wanted that boy raised by Christians like his father. Thank you, God, for leading us to Dish Land.*

"I have to check out the property lines. If Thomas' property includes the river bank, we could have a lot of cattle and we wouldn't have to pump water for them," Jacob observed.

Thomas' property. It is his property. I have been thinking of it as Jacob's and mine. What if the townspeople were wrong? What if some relatives come to take claim to Dish Land? That's ridiculous. No one would have more of a claim than a son.

There was one main store in the town. The store owner looked at the three of them and said, "You must be the people on the Martinson place. I heard you're still healthy. I couldn't believe it, but now I see it. You took on that little one, did you? Boy, come over here. I have a piece of candy for you. Come on over here; tell me which one you like."

Thomas tried to hide behind Esther's skirts, but she told him, "Thomas, if you want a piece of candy, you have to get it yourself."

Thomas went over and pointed to a bright colored piece. The store owner took it out of the glass jar with his very large hand and offered it. Thomas took the piece of candy and said, "Thank you, sir."

The man laughed and said, "You are very welcome, Thomas. You are a good boy."

"I'm Jacob Durham and this is my wife, Esther," Jacob said as he offered his hand.

As the store owner took his hand, the burly blonde man said, "Call me Pup. I was the last of ten, so that's what they called me. I don't know how to answer to anything else. I showed 'em, though; I growed up bigger'n any of 'em. What can I get for you folks today?"

Jacob said, "My wife has some things on her mind. Could you tell me who to see about the property lines out there? I don't want to be using somebody else's land."

"Elmer kin tell ya what ya need ta know. I heard there's better'n 400 acres out there. It's good to see a map, though. Elmer's been keepin' track of what the settlers are claimin' as their own, and what's Indian land. My wife and I will see to your wife's needs if you want to go there."

A short, slender young woman with black hair came into the store from a back room. She looked tired, but she smiled when she saw Esther.

"This is Esther, Rebecca. Could you help her?"

Rebecca smiled, and asked, "What is it you are looking for?"

Jacob said, "Esther, if you don't mind, I'll go see the man about the land and Thomas can stay here with you."

"That's fine," Esther agreed. She knew Jacob was not interested in her choices of dress material. "Do you have any yard goods?" she asked.

Rebecca lost her smile as she said, "We don't keep any on hand. We can show you some swatches and the order will be here in two or three weeks."

"I don't suppose you have ladies' shoes, either."

"I can take your measurements and send them to the shoemaker. That will also take a few weeks. We have some small boots on hand. Some of the ladies use those for doing chores and such."

Esther looked at her tattered shoes. *Winter is coming. I need something to cover my feet. These will be worthless in the snow.* "I'll try on some boots," Esther said reluctantly. "We'll have to wait till Jacob comes back to order shoes. I don't know if he will spend the money for shoes and boots."

Rebecca whispered to Esther, "I have been telling Pup that we need to get more things in for women, but he's afraid we won't be able to sell it all." She handed some swatches to Esther, and said, "You can order what you want, but they tend to send their own slow selling prints. They know the ladies that order are really in need and tend to keep the print that comes."

"Does the men's shirting material come as ordered?" Esther asked.

"Every time," Rebecca told her.

"It's stronger material, too," Esther observed. "Show me the latest prints that have arrived." When Rebecca pointed out the prints, Esther said, "I will order enough material for four shirts. That will make me a house dress. My husband and Thomas will get a new shirt. I found some lace and colored thread at the cabin. Some needlework will make the dress feminine. Order this print for a dress. Put a note on it that I will not accept substitutions."

Esther chose a pair of boots and a small man's winter coat she could use. Thomas stayed close to her.

When she approached the counter to order her groceries, a man with a thin face and large nose walked in. He started rattling off his order, and then he saw Esther. He stopped talking when he saw Thomas hiding behind her skirts. He stared as Esther put some of her intended purchases onto the counter.

"Wait cher turn, you dirty Injun lover!" he said. There was a lot of hate in his voice.

Esther was already angry that she had to buy men's boots for herself. Her mother's voice from years ago came softly into her anger, but another voice told her to defend herself and Thomas.

Pup said, "The lady was here first."

"Lady!? I don't see no lady! All I see is this dog and her whelp." He pointed toward Thomas. "That heathen shouldn't be allowed among decent folk!"

Esther could see that Pup was now angered, also, but she spoke for herself. "This boy's father was a Christian white man! His mother was a Christian Indian! I don't want to hear any more of your filthy lies! My husband hasn't returned from his business down the street, so I will wait for you to finish your order! If this small boy frightens you, go somewhere else!"

The man's eyes widened as he looked at Pup. "Do you .... ?"

"The **lady** said it!" Pup interrupted. "Now what is it you said you wanted?"

"I'm not scared of 'im," the man said, almost under his breath. He told Pup what he wanted and left without looking at Esther or Thomas again.

After he left, Pup looked at Esther and said, "He was wrong to say what he did, but Indians killed his brother with the family and all." After a short hesitation, Pup looked at Thomas and added, "That was some other tribe that did that deed."

Most of the groceries were collected by the time Jacob returned. He added a few things and then said, "We will be back another time for the rest. We have to carry everything on two horses."

Pup smiled and said, "The Martinson's wagon is out at the Johnson place. Nobody wanted to chance getting the sickness, so it's still there. The team of horses is grazing on their land. He must have let them go there. The house was burned to keep anybody from goin' in there like you folks did at the Martinson place. Ride north and east of the place you're in."

"Does anyone know about their family?" Jacob asked. "Who owns the place?"

"They had family back east," Pup said. "It's not like you folks, though. No one knows where to send a letter. If you want to take it over, no one will stop you. Some men went out and got the wheat crop in and took it to the mill."

"I think we have enough land for our use," Jacob told him. "The team of draft horses and wagon we need, though. I'll ride out and look things over another day. If any family shows up, tell them I would like to speak with them."

Esther said, "Jacob, we need to send a letter to our parents so they know where we are. Could we also get a writing tablet and some ink?"

"Yes, we can buy a tablet," Jacob said. "Sending a letter is good."

Pup said, "We send some letters along with our orders. Some of the mail gets through."

Esther quietly put the new purchases in the cloth sack with the rest of the things. *I am beginning to understand why Jacob's mother was so angry. She believed I convinced her son to go to California. Now she has no idea where we are, or if we are well. They will have a grandchild in the spring. I would like to share that joy with them. Even Olivia Durham's heart would be softened by her son's baby.*

12

PROTECTING HER OWN

JACOB WENT TO CHECK ON THE WAGON AND team the next day. Esther stayed home to work and to keep the fire burning. The day they went to town, they had trouble getting the fire started when they returned. Elliot had their flint. The friction stick didn't work as well. Thomas smiled broadly when Jacob saddled Joy so the boy could ride with him.

After they left, Esther spent a few minutes just absorbing the new feeling. For the first time in her life, she was absolutely alone. *There is no one I can call out to, or that can call out to me. I'm not afraid. I can talk to God. He doesn't usually speak with a voice like he did with my mother's voice, though. Being alone with God won't be so bad for one day.*

I miss my mother and everybody else we left behind. I would like to sit and visit a few minutes with any woman. So many things are happening to my body, now that I'm having a child. Jacob doesn't know about these things.

I'll clean the floors while the men folk are gone. No one will need to step on the wet floor. The wooden floors were smooth, but not varnished. She cut some lye soap into her scrub water. When she was finished cleaning the floor with a scrub brush, she got a pail of clear water to rinse it. It wouldn't do to have a soapy floor.

What would I do if they never returned? God, please don't let me have to decide that!

When Esther heard a wagon, she looked to see who it was before she allowed herself to breathe a sigh of relief. A huge team of plow horses were harnessed and hitched to the wagon. The wagon was full of hay that was held on by a hay rack. Joy and Jacob's horse, Amos, were tied behind the wagon.

Jacob was grinning as he jumped down off the wagon. "There's a tack shed and a barn over there. The harnesses were in the tack shed. There's a hay stack over there and more hay in the haymow. I can't see it all go to waste."

"I wondered how Joy and Amos would fare during the winter," Esther said. "Now we have hay to feed them."

"Next summer we'll have to make our own hay," Jacob said. "This is Oscar and Olaf. They eat hay, too."

"You named them Oscar and Olaf?" Esther asked as she laughed.

"No, Thomas told me their names. He showed me how to catch them. They like oats. There is a little of that over there, too."

Thomas stood, grinning proudly.

"I see you men folk had a good day," Esther said. "Wipe your feet before you walk on my clean floor."

"We will bring the beef cattle over before snow falls," Jacob said. "There's just a few of them. We'll need to feed them hay, too."

That evening, Esther began writing a letter. She wrote of finding the cabin, and their plans to stay and raise the boy that was born there. She told her mother of the baby she would have in the spring.

"Jacob, where are we?" When Jacob looked at her quizzically, Esther added, "What is the name of this place? I want to tell my mother and Kara and Ira where we are."

Jacob looked a bit sheepish as he said, "We're in the north part of the state of Iowa."

"Iowa! That's far north of the trail we planned to follow on Elliot's map!"

"That's true. He said he wanted to take the northern route to California. We went a little too far north."

"Jacob, I'll have to pray for that man. He is even more helpless than I thought. How is he going to survive alone?"

"He'll find someone to help him out," Jacob said, confidently, "he always does."

Esther decided to drop the subject, but she continued to be concerned for their friend.

"Jacob," she said. "You need to write to your mother and father, too. We can put it all in one envelope, but your parents will want to hear from you."

Jacob sat thoughtfully, and then he came over to the table. "I want to tell my brothers about this farmland. You don't have to clear the land. It's the best farm land I have ever seen. It's one big pasture. You write it for me, Esther."

"That message is not going to be in my handwriting," Esther told him with conviction. "Your mother hates me for taking you away. I won't take the blame for enticing your brothers away from her."

"My mother can't blame you for that! Why do you think that?"

"She told me." As Jacob continued to stare at her, she added, "On our wedding day, she told me that I was leaving because of my bad reputation. She thinks I convinced you to leave with me."

"I can't believe she said that to you, but if you say she did, she did. You have never lied to me." Jacob took the pen Esther offered, and began to write. "What did you do to get a bad reputation?"

Esther was going to explain how she believed she got on his mother's bad side when she noticed that Jacob was smiling. "I was a bad influence on Leah," she joked back.

"I think my little sister will be a spinster. My mother won't let any possible suitors get close."

"Leah knows how to get around your mother," Esther said. "If she sees a man she likes, she'll find a way."

As Jacob finished his letter, he said. "We'll send this off right away. Maybe in the spring, we'll hear an answer."

The fall work was unrelenting and hard. Jacob and Esther put the potatoes, carrots, and squash into the root cellar. Jacob showed her how to cut the cabbage and put it into the sauerkraut crock. They made a three-sided shelter of sod so the livestock would have a break from the wind.

Each night, Esther went to bed bone tired. Sometimes, she fell asleep in the middle of her prayers.

Jacob went to cut some wood by the river one day. He took the draft team and wagon. Thomas went with him, riding Joy, so he could ride back to get some of the fresh bread Esther was making for their lunch. When Esther heard horses, she was alert to the fact that it probably wouldn't be Jacob. She put her holster and gun on under her apron before she went to the door.

This time it was a group of soldiers approaching. She did not relax; however, as she noticed that one soldier was leading Joy. Thomas was being held on the saddle with another soldier.

The sergeant called a halt and spoke to her. "We found an Injun on this horse out there, ma'am. Did he steal it from you?"

"The horse is mine, but Thomas has my permission to ride her," Esther called out. "Let him go! He belongs here."

"We have our orders to pick up any stray hostiles. He belongs on Indian land. If you let him ride your horse, ma'am, he'll take it back to the tribe and you won't see it, again."

Thomas was trying to get away, but the soldier said, "You sit still or I'll put your neck in a noose."

Esther drew her gun. "Let Thomas go, now!" she told the man. She aimed toward the sergeant.

"You ain't gonna shoot me over an Injun brat?" the sergeant said. "We've got ten guns to your one."

Esther considered what he said to her. She noticed the beautiful horse the sergeant was riding. "No, I won't shoot you. I'll shoot your horse! You are on our land. You have my horse. Let the boy bring that horse back to me, now! If you shoot me, you'll have to explain why you shot a pregnant white woman on her own step."

"Let 'im go," the sergeant said. "One little brat ain't worth the trouble."

Thomas got down and took hold of Joy's lead. The soldier holding it hesitated, then let go of the lead. When the horse and Thomas were beside her, Esther lowered her gun.

The sergeant spoke again. "Well, little lady, I don't think you know much about shootin' that thing. You could'a shot one of my men if you pulled the trigger."

"I won't waste the ammunition showing you how well I can shoot," Esther told him. "Don't bother this boy, again. His father was white. He isn't hostile."

"Oh, a breed, is he? He'll be trouble for ya. You got a man to protect you?" the sergeant said as he looked around.

"My husband and I protect each other. We both protect this boy."

The sergeant grunted in response, and then he yelled, "Move out!"

After the sergeant turned away, the other soldiers saluted Esther as they rode past.

Esther and Thomas watched as the soldiers rode away. When they were nearly out of sight, Thomas asked, "Where were they going to take me?"

"I don't know, but you belong here," Esther told him.

Thomas tied Joy to the hitching post and said, "Is lunch ready?"

Esther walked back into her kitchen. She put together the lunch she had prepared with shaking hands. *Thomas doesn't look as though he was affected by the threat. I hope by the time he grows up there will be less hate for him. He is Thomas, not just a half breed. He's a smart little boy. I can't believe I told ten strange men that I am pregnant. A lady does not talk of such things in mixed company. Here on the prairie I have to do and say things I never thought I would.*

†

The winter brought deep snow that made it impossible to drive the team to town. The three of them were confined to their little space in the cabin most of the time. Jacob had his outside chores to do each day, giving the animals hay, but that did not take long.

Esther spent a lot of time sewing for all of them. Esther made baby things of cotton flannel. There was colored thread in the cabin that she used to embroider the tiny things. She was finally grateful for her training in stitchery. Esther also kept the baby things that Summer made. She wondered if she would use them, but she couldn't bear to throw the beautiful beaded work away.

Esther was beginning to hate looking out from the inside of the cabin. She would have to melt the leafy patterned frost off the window to see out at all. It was as though the cabin had changed from the home she loved to a jail cell. *How can I be so tired of seeing my husband's face? This is the same man I couldn't wait to be with. I don't want to get away from him forever. I just want to go out and visit with someone else for a little while.*

Jacob helped grind the dried corn by hand. Esther could tell that he, too, felt confined.

One sunny day Jacob came in carrying wood and saying, "It's warm out there. I think I'll go hunting. I'd like some fresh meat for supper."

"Fresh meat sounds good," Esther told him. "I wish I could go out, too."

Jacob looked at her and said, "You know you can't go out on horseback in your condition."

"I know, and I'm tired of the vegetable diet, too. I'll stay here and grind some more corn into corn meal. Good luck with hunting," Esther told Jacob. She watched with a bit of envy as Jacob saddled his horse and rode off in a zigzag path. The snow had drifted, so he rode in the spaces between drifts where the snow was not as deep.

Thomas said, "He won't even find a prairie chicken."

"Maybe he'll find some kind of fresh meat," she told him as she turned to go back inside.

Esther went about her work till after noon. The wood that Jacob had brought in was getting low, so she went out to get more. *At least Jacob isn't here to tell me I can't carry wood. Carrying wood in isn't any worse than going to the outhouse on a cold morning. Frost clings to the edge of the hole where my bottom melts it off when I sit down.*

"Come on, Thomas, lets get wood in before we run out," she said. To her surprise, she found a freshly killed young pheasant hanging from the hitching post. She looked around for Jacob, but he was nowhere to be seen. "Jacob!?" she called. She looked at the tracks in the snow. She saw what she thought might be moccasin tracks.

Thomas came out and watched her as she was trying to decide where the tracks led. "Mother's people," he said. He took hold of the pheasant. He was walking toward the cabin when Esther stopped him.

"We have to dress it out, first," she told him. "Bring it over by the wood pile, out of the wind. I'll get a knife." Esther saved the feathers for use, later. She took out the entrails as she had done with chickens many times before.

Jacob came home just before dark. He carried the saddle in and announced, "The only thing I saw was a skunk. I didn't think you wanted me to bring that home."

Esther and Thomas laughed as they watched Jacob sniff the air. His eyes widened as he asked, "What's that good smell?"

"You'll see," Esther told him. "Wait till supper is done." She smiled as she was thoroughly enjoying the secret that she and Thomas shared. *I have so few opportunities to surprise Jacob.*

"It smells like chicken, but just a little different."

When she lifted the cover of the cast iron roaster, the delicious smell permeated the air. "It's bigger'n a prairie chicken," Jacob said. "It has to be a pheasant. How did you get a pheasant? I didn't even find a track."

Thomas laughed with Esther as they watched him wonder. Thomas said, "Mother's people know how to catch pheasant."

"Summer's people must have left it," Esther finally told him. "It was on the hitching post. I didn't even hear them come. I saw a few moccasin tracks, but that's all."

As they enjoyed the meal, Jacob said, "Thomas, we will have to remember your mother's people when we have plenty."

Thomas simply nodded. He was not a chatty boy.

As spring grew closer, Esther tried to tell Jacob about what he would need to do for her when she went into labor.

He simply said, "I've pulled a lot of calves. People can't be much different."

"Jacob, you can't pull a baby like you do with a calf! You'll cripple the baby for life."

Esther was beginning to wonder if Thomas might be more help to her. "Maybe there's a midwife in town," Esther said aloud. "I surely hope there is."

Jacob said, "I'll ride to town after the thaw. I'll ask after a midwife. I know there's no doctor."

God, please don't let this baby be born till after the spring thaw. And help us find a good midwife.

13

NEW BIRTH

JACOB RODE TO TOWN ALONE WHEN THE BARE ground could be seen. Esther desperately wanted to go with him, but he wouldn't allow it.

"I rode up and checked the road," he said. "The wagon would get stuck in the mud and you're not going on horseback in your condition."

Esther and Thomas walked about the yard, checking for green grass where the snow melted. Mainly they were just enjoying the fresh air. They had to take care when stepping out the door, as the thawing snow had left a small lake of water. *Mr. Martinson should have placed the cabin a little higher. The dish kept the winter wind from blowing quite so hard against the cabin, but if there is more melting snow it might flood.*

Joy followed Esther, expecting a treat of a carrot or a bit of oats. "You are spoiled, you know that don't you," Esther told her as she hugged her neck. Esther put her hands on Joy's back and onto her belly. "Oooh, Joy. You have a colt under that winter coat! We're both due to have a baby this spring. I suppose that Jacob will just say he knew it all along. Where did you find a father for your baby?"

Thomas didn't say anything, but he grinned broadly as if he knew something.

"Can we thank your mother's people for providing a stallion for Joy?" Esther asked him.

Thomas continued to grin, but still said nothing.

"Well, we'll have to wait and see what this colt looks like," Esther said.

†

"We will have green grass soon," Esther said aloud. "I am so hungry for some fresh food from the garden. When the ground thaws, we can dig parsnips."

Thomas got a quizzical look on his face.

As Esther continued with her walk, she talked of more things she saw about to happen with the coming of spring. She paused to sigh deeply, taking in the fresh air.

Thomas said, "We are here. The air is warm. What's wrong with now?"

Esther stood quietly for a moment. "I think you're right, Thomas. Sometimes I think about the future so much, I fail to appreciate what I have now. I should be thanking God for this warm air. We have to have some dreams for the future, though. That's what keeps us going. I just shouldn't forget to feel what's good, now."

Thomas listened intently, and then smiled as though he agreed.

†

Jacob came home with a big smile on his face.

"I hope that grin means you found a midwife," Esther told him.

"I did. She'll be out to see you as soon as she can get through on the road." Jacob gave her a hug before he took the saddle off his horse.

"You've been drinking!" Esther said incredulously, as she smelled the distinctive odor. She had never known him to drink any more than a glass of wine or beer.

"I have a famous wife," Jacob told her. "Everywhere I went, I heard about the woman that held a gun on Sergeant Stevens. The story goes that the men with the sergeant told the whole story in the bar about how this little woman made their sergeant back down. Pup wanted to buy me a drink. He told me the men in town wanted to meet me. That sergeant is well known. He's always stickin' his nose in other people's business."

"What did you tell **them**?" Esther asked.

Jacob's words were slurring as he answered, "I said that sergeant was a wise man. He knew when to retreat. My wife could outshoot him any day."

"You didn't!?" Esther said, incredulously.

"I told them Sergeant Stevens was lucky to get out of here alive."

Esther shook her head. "You didn't tell them I shot two men, did you?"

"No, I din't have to tell 'em that. They figgered it out. I told em you protec' your own. Just ask the two guys that tried to steal your horse."

"Jacob, I think you need to sober up before we continue this discussion. I hope we don't have a Sergeant Stevens on our doorstep with his gun in hand."

"We won' see 'im. He put in for a transfer."

"How do you know that?"

"Sojers talk." Jacob let out a loud burp.

†

A few days later the midwife arrived as promised. She sat in her buggy and asked, "Am I going to be sick if I go in your house?"

"I cleaned every part of this cabin last winter," Esther assured her. "The smallpox is gone."

"I'm Fiona Grey," she said, as she removed her bright yellow gingham bonnet from her graying brown hair. The woman looked strong with her stocky build. She didn't look fat, just square. "You look healthier than most of my spring mothers," Fiona commented.

"I haven't been very sick, and we had vegetables from Summer's garden to eat all winter," Esther explained.

"Summer? Oh, the Indian woman. I would have come out for her, but she didn't want anyone to help her. Maybe it's good I didn't come, seein' she got sick and all. I would have been dead and gone by now."

"Have a chair," Esther said, "I'll take your shawl. I haven't had any visitors, yet, so I'm forgetting my manners."

"I hope you know that the ladies would have all made a time to pay a welcome call, but they were afraid," Fiona said. "They can't believe you are still alive, comin' in here on the sickness like you did. And now you're havin' a little one. God be praised!"

"My husband and I were both vaccinated. That's why we didn't get smallpox. I wouldn't want people to visit and spread smallpox all over town. You can tell them there is no danger."

Esther made coffee and set out the cookies she had made.

"Land sakes, you have been doing well! You've been baking cookies, too. That's the biggest cook stove I ever laid eyes on. They don't come any bigger'n that."

"I cooked on a stove half again that size in the hotel where I grew up."

"How'd they get it through the door?"

"I suppose they put it together in the room. It was there ever since I could remember."

"Well, aren't you the one?"

Fiona just looked at Esther for a minute as though deciding whether to believe her. "Well, I like to see where you plan to give birth."

"That will do nicely," Fiona said when Esther led her into the bedroom. "Now we should discuss what might be happening to tell you to send your husband to get me."

"I believe I know the signs of labor," Esther told her. "I just need some experienced help during labor."

"This isn't your first baby?"

"It's my first baby, but I was with a friend when the doctor told her about the signs of labor and they were listed in a medical book I read."

Fiona's eyes widened. "You have a medical book?"

"The doctor loaned me one to read after I helped with the people sick with smallpox in the hotel."

"Woman, is there no end to what you can do? I heard you are some kind of sharp shooter that scared off that awful Sergeant Stevens. Now you tell me you know some about doctorin'."

"I didn't exactly scare him off."

"Well, he's gone. That's good. The way I heard it, he couldn't take the way his troops laughed at him. Folks around here have tried tell that man to leave that little river tribe alone. They don't attack anyone. They might decide to attack somebody if he didn't stop pesterin' 'em."

"He was planning to carry off Thomas to who knows where," Esther told her. "He also had my horse. That's why I drew a gun on him."

"Are you as good with that gun as I heard talk of?"

"My husband won that gun in a shooting contest. We are about equal in shooting ability. I haven't practiced for a long time, because I don't have the extra bullets to play around with."

"You better get 'em," Fiona told her. "I heard talk about some renegades from the other tribes killin' off settlers."

"Don't tell me that, Fiona, I was just starting to feel safe."

"It's better to be on your guard. If you see painted faces, that's war paint. When you see war paint, get your gun."

"You're right; I should get more ammunition, but let's get back to talking about the baby before the men folk come back. I do have some questions for you. I haven't had a woman to talk with all winter. When I finally get a woman within earshot, I don't want to spend our time talking about guns."

"I was startin' to think you knew all about it. Maybe you didn't need me at all."

"Those medical books are written by men, so how do they know?"

"You are so right. We women are the ones with the burdens. The men just sit around and look proud," Fiona said, laughing. The two talked for hours till Fiona said she had to get home.

One day the weather was so warm that Esther opened up the windows to let the fresh air into the cabin. She cleaned the winter dust off from everything till she went to bed, exhausted.

In the morning, she awoke to find that Jacob was already out of bed. As she got up, fluid leaked out. She called out, "Jacob! .... Jacob?! .... Thomas??! She could hear Jacob's voice, faintly. She walked to the door and saw Jacob and Thomas out by the sod shed. "Jacob!" she called.

"I can't come in," he said. "Joy's having a foal!"

"You have to ride for the midwife! I'm having the baby!"

"I can't leave now! Joy's having her foal!"

I can't believe my ears! My husband won't ride for the midwife, because he has to stay with a horse! I love Joy as much as anyone, but I want that midwife here! "Jacob! Come over here so we can talk!"

"I'll be there in a minute. I think Joy's in trouble."

Esther closed the door and went to get the bed ready. She felt pressure in her abdomen.

Jacob ran into the house, tracking mud as he went. "I have to get back out there!" he said.

"I'm leaking fluid, so I am definitely in labor. You have to get the midwife, now!"

"Thomas can ride for the midwife. I have to stay with Joy."

"Thomas is just a little boy!"

"He can do it, can't you boy?"

Thomas nodded.

"You ride to town. The first house you come to is the midwife," Jacob told him.

"He's never ridden your horse before. What if he throws him?"

"He won't throw him. He'll have that midwife back here as fast as I could. I hate to lose our first foal. We might even lose Joy."

Jacob grabbed his saddle. Esther could hear the hoof beats as Thomas rode away. Esther used the chamber pot inside for the first time. She didn't want to go outside, as she might not be able to get back in under her own power. *My husband is too busy to see to my needs. Oh, the labor pains are getting stronger.*

The midwife had not arrived when Jacob came into the house and said, "We have a little filly. Her left leg and up onto her chest is white. She has spots of brown and white all over the rest of her. I've never seen a horse like it! I didn't even know she had a foal on board. All our horses are gelded, so where did she find a stallion?"

"Thomas and I noticed it a few weeks ago," Esther said. "I've seen a horse just like that." Esther was gritting her teeth in pain.

"When did you see a stallion like that?" Jacob asked.

"Go wash the horse off your hands," Esther told him. "You may have to deliver this baby next."

Jacob stood there with his mouth open, and then he said, "The midwife told me first babies can take a full day to be born."

"Most do, but I don't think this one will," Esther said quickly.

Jacob grabbed the lye soap and filled the basin to wash. He took off his soiled shirt before washing.

"Who has a stallion like that?" Jacob asked again, as he dried off.

"One of the men who came to get Summer's body was riding a horse just like you described."

Between pains, Esther went to the door to find out if she could see the new foal. The little foal was nursing. *She is just like the horse I saw that day. Joy, you found a handsome father for your baby!*

Esther lay on the bed to prepare for the birth. Jacob began pacing around the bedroom. When Esther had a short moment between pains, she said, "Get a chair and sit down! You're upsetting me with that useless walking about!"

Esther was having a strong pain when Fiona breezed into the room. "I knew I had to hurry when you sent the boy to fetch me!" she said. "That Thomas is quite the boy. He even helped me hitch up the buggy. My man was at the store."

Esther couldn't reply. She had a pushing pain. Minutes later the baby girl was placed on her abdomen. She let out one cry, and then moved her little hands as if searching for something to hold.

"I can't believe all that was inside of me!" Esther said.

"All that and more," Fiona told her.

Jacob stood wide eyed as he watched his newborn daughter.

Fiona tied and cut the cord. She wrapped the tiny baby and gave her to Jacob while she cleaned the area. "Take that little one in there by the kitchen stove," she told Jacob. "She needs to be kept warm. I'll be out to clean her up in a minute or two."

Jacob was talking softly to the baby as he walked out of the room. "You're going to be a strong lady, just like your mother," he said.

Esther closed her eyes, exhausted, as Fiona went about her work. "I'll be here till she's on her feet and doin' for herself," she heard Fiona tell Jacob.

Later that afternoon, Fiona asked Esther if she would like to sit at the table to eat. "Some of 'em are up to it," she told Esther. "You're about as strong as they come." Esther didn't think that was true, but she decided to take the compliment, anyway. Fiona stood by as Esther took her first few steps.

After eating lunch, Fiona brought out a journal. "Jacob said you haven't settled on a name. As soon as you do, write the name and April 25th, 1850. Put it right there on that clean page.

"You don't write in your own journal?" Esther asked.

Fiona blushed. "I never learned to read or write. My father said that women keep house, so they have no need of learnin'. Most babies have one person in the family that can write the name in. I take it to the courthouse and they write it in their book. My girls go to school, so they won't be ignorant like their mother."

"Don't call yourself ignorant just because you didn't have the opportunity to learn!" Esther told her. "Look at all you've learned. You help young mothers have their babies. No reading person could have been more help to me."

"Let's get a name for this beautiful baby," Fiona said, quickly, as if she was uncomfortable with praise.

Esther looked at Thomas and Jacob. This cabin was built for Summer. Thomas, what do you think of the name Evangeline Summer Durham?"

For the first time, Esther saw a look of surprise come over Thomas' face.

"Evangeline means angel, so it seems right to me," Esther continued.

Thomas nodded.

"Are you sure?" Esther said. "We should all agree. This will be her name forever."

Thomas nodded again.

Jacob said, "Evangeline was my grandmother's name. I like that. It's good that we remember Summer, too."

Fiona handed the journal to Jacob. He wrote the name and date on the page.

"Now write the mother's name and the father's name," Fiona said. When Fiona took the book back, she marked the page with a crocheted cross.

14

STRONG MEDICINE WOMAN

WHEN EVANGELINE WAS TWO MONTHS OLD, JACOB AND Esther decided the time had come for the mother and baby to go to town. Esther dressed Eve in her best dress. She put on her own best skirt and blouse.

"Maybe we could speak to a minister about having her baptized." Esther said.

"Yes, that too," Jacob said. "Bring your gun. We'll check on getting some bullets for it."

They all got into the wagon for the trip to town. Esther gave Thomas an old blanket to sit on as the wagon had only one seat.

"Eve likes the jiggling of the wagon," Esther said, as the baby went to sleep as they rode to town.

Pup smiled broadly when he saw them enter the store. "Rebecca!" he called. "The Durham's baby is here!" He said to Jacob, "She's been telling me she wants to see that baby. If I didn't tell her as soon as you got here, she'd pick me up and hang me by my heels."

Esther laughed at the picture of anyone being able to pick up the huge man, much less his tiny wife. "She's not that strong," she said.

Rebecca came into the room. "Could I hold her?" she asked.

"Please do," Esther said, "She's little, but I've had her in my arms for quite awhile. She is beginning to feel heavy."

Rebecca took the baby and opened her thin cotton blanket. "So this is what a baby girl looks like! She's as delicate as a flower! I have three boys. I should have known I wouldn't have a daughter when I married a man with nine brothers."

"Pup is the youngest of ten boys? I can't imagine having that many boys!"

"I can't believe I had three," Rebecca said. "One child takes all your time and energy. When you have more, you just do it."

Jacob called out that he was going down the street to talk to a man about a cow. "I'll be right here," Esther told him. Esther turned back to Rebecca and said, "You can only do so much work. I used to think that if I had a home and a husband, I wouldn't have to work so hard. I have learned that I was wrong."

"You didn't have a home?"

"My father died before I was born. All my life, my mother and I worked in a hotel. We lived in a back room. I thought I worked harder than anyone else in the world. I didn't appreciate all the work that was done for me. My meals were provided. There was always milk, eggs, garden produce and meat delivered. Yard boys brought in wood. When I worked as a cook, I cooked for as many as 50 people. I thought cooking for two or three people would be so easy. Now I have to do it all or do without."

"I have to work in the store a lot, but you are right about some things," Rebecca said. "I have milk and eggs delivered, and Mrs. Thompson brings vegetables in season. Women have to work. I haven't met anyone, man, woman or child who doesn't work hard out here on the plains," Rebecca said.

"Little baby girls are a lot of work, too," Esther told her, as she smiled.

"I believe you. I just want to find out for myself when we have this one."

"Oh, it's so nice to hear some good news like that! Well, you can practice holding mine for a while. Maybe it will help."

Rebecca said, "While I hold her, you can look at the yard goods we have in stock."

"All ready to buy?"

"They are ready to buy. Pup finally let me order some to keep in stock. We have more families coming in all the time. Some are just traveling through on their way to Oregon, but they need new dresses by the time they get this far. Come over here and look."

"Most of my clothes were in tatters by the time we got here," Esther said, nodding as they walked to the yard goods. "I don't know when I'll get time to sew, but the baby is growing so fast, I might have to take time to make her some bigger dresses. Oh, I like your choices!" Esther said, as she looked at the material.

"I decided that just because our ladies live in the wilderness, they shouldn't have to wear ugly dresses."

"Good for you! We all thank you," Esther said.

As Esther said that, she heard a horse riding fast, close to the front door. She also heard the noise of something breaking coming from the area of the back room. As she looked out the window, she could see the spotted stallion that she had seen before, but the Indian that dismounted was not the same one.

Thomas said, "War paint. He's an enemy."

It took Esther a few seconds to take in the implications of what Thomas said. The Indian came into the store with a tomahawk in hand. He covered the distance from the door to the counter in a flash. Two more Indians came in from the back room.

Pup reacted, quickly. He took a pistol out from under the counter and shot the first Indian. Esther could see blood coming from Pup's upper right arm. Esther had her pistol out of the holster. *I have to be sure I don't hit Pup. We'll all be killed if I don't shoot. I hope they aren't Summer's people.*

She shot once, and one Indian staggered and fell. The other one turned his attention toward her, looking surprised. She shot again, and watched the other Indian take two steps before falling. Two more Indians were coming in the door.

Pup had reloaded by this time, so he shot one of those two. Esther shot the other.

Another Indian came partway into the door. He saw the fallen Indians. He looked straight at Esther. He turned to yell something out the door. Esther thought he might leave. She shot, anyway. That Indian staggered outside, yelling the same words before he fell.

Rifle shots could be heard on the street. Pup got a rifle and peeked out the door.

He shot the rifle, once, and then turned his attention to the bleeding Indians. The one that had attacked Pup was making gurgling noises as he breathed. Pup shot him, again. "We don't need any half dead ones," he said. "They were after our guns and ammunition. We just got some in stock."

"We have to check on the boys," Rebecca said in a shaky whisper.

"Boys!" Pup yelled. "Come down here and be counted." He went into the back room where the stairs were and yelled again.

There were no more rifle shots to be heard.

Noise on the stairs indicated the boys were coming down. The three boys, three different sizes, looked extra small, standing next to Pup. They looked scared, but intact. The youngest was just a toddler. "I found these three comin' down the stairs," Pup said, "They look like ours."

"How can you joke at a time like this?" Rebecca asked Pup, incredulously, with her voice still shaking.

Esther took her crying baby, although her whole body was trembling, so Rebecca could go to her own children. "Pup, that arm needs attention," Esther said.

He looked at the bleeding arm. "Come to think of it, that thing does hurt."

Suddenly, Esther thought of Jacob down the street. She started toward the door, but Jacob burst through the door, wide eyed. When he saw Esther and the baby, he relaxed in relief.

Esther went to him with the baby in her arms. Thomas was right behind her. They did a group hug. Esther was crying and shaking.

Jacob said, "I saw the Indians with war paint going in, but I had to get the ones on the street first, before I could come. I didn't know if I would find you alive."

Esther tried to comfort her crying baby, but she couldn't stop crying herself.

Pup spoke up, "None of us would be alive if Esther wasn't here. How many guns are you hiding in that skirt, ma'am?"

"Just one," Esther told him with her voice shaking.

"Nobody can reload that fast," Pup said.

"It's a new type of gun called a revolver," Jacob told him. "It shoots six bullets before you have to reload."

"I need one of them," Pup said. "Could I see it?"

Esther put the gun into Pup's hand. Pup winced in pain. "Pup, we need to clean that wound and dress it, so you don't get infection. You can still die if that wound gets infected."

"I can't get my mind around this," Pup said. "You save my life with your gun, and yer talkin' like a doctor?"

"Somebody has to do it, Pup," Esther said, "You're still bleeding. Take your shirt off. We'll get this done." She handed the baby to Jacob.

Esther cleaned the wound with cooled water from the teakettle that had been sitting on the heating stove. "See, this material from your shirt is in the wound. If we didn't take it out, the wound wouldn't heal," Esther told him.

Rebecca cut some new flannel to bind up the wound. When she finished, Pup picked up the tomahawk that had done the damage. "I'm going to save this," he said. He hung it on the wall behind the counter. "When I see that, I'll remember this day."

"God saved us all from these enemies," Esther said. She looked at the painted faces that Fiona had warned her about. *I wonder if their mothers are alive to cry for them. They don't look so dangerous, now.* She took the baby from her husband's arms. "Could I go to a quiet place to sit so I can feed her? That might calm her down."

Rebecca led her upstairs to the living area above the store. "Don't mind the mess," she said. "Pup has needed me to mind the store, so I don't get my own work done."

She showed Esther to a rocking chair. Esther rocked and fed the baby till Eve finally fell asleep. "That rocking chair was just what we needed," Esther whispered. "Eve and I are both a lot calmer, now."

When Rebecca and Esther went back downstairs, the bodies were gone. Pup was cleaning the blood off the floor.

"Well, we should get the things we came to buy," Esther said. "We don't want to do this again tomorrow."

"You get some bullets for that gun, no charge," Pup said. "And what else do you see around here that you want?"

"She likes our rocking chair," Rebecca said.

"It's yours," Pup said. "Every little baby needs some rocking."

"I can't take your own rocker," Esther told them.

"We'll order a new one," Pup said. "It'll be here before our next one pops out."
Rebecca blushed.

"I'll take the rocker," Esther said, "but we'll pay for it the next time we come into town. That's an expensive chair."

Pup said, "I'll order an easy chair for Jacob, too. He needs one for the long cold winter."

As they left the store, the townspeople stared unashamedly. One man came up to them and shook Jacob's hand. "I'm Chadwick Olson. All of us are beholden to both of you," he said. "If there's anything we can do for you, let us know. If the two of you hadn't acted so quickly, I hate to think what would have happened. Ma'am, do you mind me askin' where you learned to shoot like that?"

"Jacob taught me," Esther said. "I didn't have a parlor for him to court me in, so he took me out to the shooting range to practice. He won the pistol at a shooting contest."

"We are grateful you decided to come to our town," Mr. Olson said.

"We were protecting ourselves, too," Jacob said.

Esther saw the spotted stallion, still standing on the street. "Let's take that stallion home," Esther told Jacob.

Mr. Olson and another man close by jumped at the task of tying the horse to the wagon. "The spoils of war," Mr. Olson said.

"Do you have a minister in town?" Esther asked. "We want to get this baby baptized."

"We have a traveling minister that comes through once a month. We'll send him out to you when he comes," one of the other men said.

They drove out of town with the rocking chair rocking in the wagon and the spotted stallion following. Thomas was somber faced as he looked at the stallion.

Esther waited till they were out of town before she said, "Jacob, that horse belonged to Summer's people. He must have been stolen from them."

"I'll take him over to the camp by the river, tomorrow," he said.

"Yes, we had enough excitement for one day," Esther said. "Thank God, we weren't hurt." *I don't think Summer's people would give up this beautiful stallion without a fight. I think they lost the fight.*

Esther was glad to be home at the cabin. Jacob put some kindling wood on the smoldering peat fire. They had learned that peat would keep a fire going longer. Esther put Eve into her cradle. She gratefully watched her sleep a moment before she walked back into the great room. "Thomas," she asked, quietly, "Could you understand what that Indian said when he yelled out the door?"

"He warned the others," Thomas told her. When Esther continued to look at him, Thomas added, "He said, 'The woman with strong medicine is here.'"

Jacob and Esther looked at each other. Esther asked, "What does that mean?"

"It means you have great power over your enemies," Thomas said as though he couldn't believe she didn't know.

"We had to shoot those Indians," Jacob told Thomas.

"I know. They are enemies of the River People. The River People are dead."

"We'll ride over there, tomorrow," Jacob promised. "We'll find out what happened."

"They are dead," Thomas said, again. "The horse told me."

"I'm sorry, Thomas," Esther said. "They were good people."

Jacob shook his head at her simple acceptance of Thomas' belief. He went outside to bring in the rocking chair.

Esther decided not to try to explain to him how the horse had told her and Thomas about the death of Summer's people. *Jacob doesn't understand. Sometimes you just know things. He'll have to ride over and see for himself.*

The next day, the baby was extra fussy while Jacob was gone. Thomas was invited along, but he said he would stay home. "I'll watch for enemies," he said.

Esther told Jacob, "Thomas warned me about those Indians as they ran in. I might have been slower to shoot if he hadn't warned me."

Thomas beamed with pride, although he still looked sad.

Jacob came home with a somber look about him. He said nothing till the team was set free and the harness was hung up. When he was ready, he simply said, "Thomas was right."

"Thomas, you are the only one left," Esther told him. "You have a special mission to carry on for your mother's family."

"I can't do it," Thomas replied. "I am only one."

"You're right, Thomas," Jacob said, thoughtfully. "A man has to be what he is and no more."

Later, as they lay in bed, Jacob told Esther, "There wasn't a single usable thing left in that camp. Everything was smashed, burned, or carried off. They might have carried off some of the women and children, but I saw a lot of dead ones. The bodies I saw had spots on them. They looked like they had the measles."

Esther was thoughtful, and then she said. "If none of them had the measles when they were young, all of them would get sick. They were sick; that's why they were defeated."

"They may think they had a great victory," Jacob told her, "but this time the spoils come with the measles."

"You mean the enemy tribe will get the measles. That sounds like justice. Summer's tribe may have died at the hand of the warring tribe, but they were really killed by the white man's disease."

"You can't blame white people for what I saw," Jacob replied, with anger in his voice.

"You're right. It's sad that the friendly Indians get killed by the warring tribes," Esther decided.

"We're lucky that we have the *strong medicine woman* to protect us," Jacob said.

Esther laughed. "Your mother was right. My reputation is following me. You'll have to write her so she knows what my reputation is now."

"We should be getting a letter from our families, soon," Jacob said. If we don't hear in a month, we'll send another letter."

I should tell Jacob about hearing and seeing my mother, but he wouldn't understand. I am allowed one secret. Sometimes, I feel like God sends her to protect me, but how can that be?

God, help me stop shaking inside so I can rest. Watch over us and protect us while we sleep.

15

GOOD NEWS AND...

THE SUMMER WAS PASSING VERY QUICKLY. THE WORK Esther had to do was growing as fast as her baby. She kept the garden weeded as well as doing her other housework. Some of the townspeople had given her their extra seed to add to the seed she had saved. She now had radishes and lettuce in season. She had string beans and peas to pick. Eve was put on a blanket on the grass while Esther worked in the garden.

Church services were held in the school each Sunday. The traveling minister gave a sermon when he was there. On the day Eve was baptized, Fiona played a homemade stringed instrument that she laid flat on her lap as she sang. Eve's eyes widened when the music began. As the song flowed throughout the room, Esther realized that Eve had never heard music. The baby smiled and Esther was grateful to hear a melody. *I hope you can learn music when you grow up*, Esther said to herself.

After the service, Esther sought out Fiona. "I loved your song. How did you learn music?"

"My grandfather taught me," Fiona said. "He came to live with us after my grandmother died. On winter days, he showed all of us the tunes he knew. I like to remember the old ones."

Esther smiled and said, "Do you remember when you told me you were ignorant?"

"Well, I am," Fiona said, quickly. "I can't read a thing."

"If you are ignorant, then I am, too, because I don't know music," Esther told her.

"Oh, hush!" Fiona said, "I won't hear any more of that nonsense!"

"Thank you so much for singing so beautifully today," Esther told her. "I miss hearing music. I wish one of us had learned to play an instrument. Your song was a special blessing."

Fiona blushed, but smiled at the compliment. "Any singin' to the glory of the Lord is a special blessing."

The next week, Esther did her work with a happier heart. Tunes from the past were revisiting her, as though music was reawakened in her soul.

This day, Esther had heated water to wash clothes and the baby's diapers. The wash could be done outside during warm weather. That way she didn't have to be so careful of spilling water. She scrubbed everything clean on a washboard and rinsed them well before hanging them out to dry. Esther's hands were scrubbed raw when she finished. She saw a grey cloud on the horizon. *Cloud, you had better not come here till my wash is dry. I don't want rain spots on my laundry after all that work!*

She dumped the wash water away from the cabin. Before she went into the cabin to start supper, she heard the sound of a wagon approaching. Jacob was just outside, so he stood with her to watch the approach.

Thomas stood by Jacob and said, "The man is our enemy."

As the wagon drew closer, Esther saw that, indeed it was the man who had called Thomas a heathen and had called her a dog. He had a woman with him on the wagon seat.

As the man stopped the team, he spoke to Jacob. "I would like you to help my son." He got down off the wagon and offered his hand. "My son has blisters all over him. In town they told me this was the only place I might find help for him. They said you have some kind of power over this sickness." He pointed to Thomas. "You saved that boy there, and you didn't get sick."

The man glanced at Esther and Thomas, but kept his gaze on Jacob. Jacob pointed to Esther and said, "You'll have to speak to my wife. Esther's the one with the medical knowledge."

The man lowered his eyes momentarily. Reluctantly, he turned to Esther and said, "I know you have no reason to help me, but **please** think about my son. He is covered with blisters. We're afraid we'll all die of this sickness."

"Could you tell us what to do?" the woman asked from her perch on the wagon seat.

"I won't invite you in," Esther said. The three of us won't get smallpox, but I have a baby. She is not protected against it. I will look at the boy, but I won't touch him."

A boy's head popped out of the covered wagon. When the woman saw him, she said, "You get back there and lay down! You need your rest!"

The tension went out of Esther as she saw the boy. "Let him come out," she said.

The parent's eyes widened and Jacob held his breath.

"Stand right there by your mother," Esther told the boy. "How old are you?"

"I'm eight years old tomorrow," he said joyfully. His voice was clear, without hesitation. There were blisters on his face, but not all around his mouth.

"Where did you find your first blisters? Show me," Esther told him.

The boy lifted up his shirt to reveal scratched sores on his chest.

"Don't scratch those sores open," Esther told him. She looked at the concerned mother. "He'll be fine. He doesn't have smallpox, he has chickenpox."

"You can't know that!" the man said, angrily.

"Your son is talking without pain. That means he doesn't have blisters in his mouth and throat. He isn't sick enough to have smallpox. Keep him from scratching the blisters. He could get infection in the blisters if he scratches them open. A little baking soda in his bath water will help the itching."

"I don't have any at home," the mother said. "We'll have to buy some."

"They won't let us back in town," the man said with anger in his voice. "You heard 'em say that!"

"Thomas," Esther said, "Would you get the extra container of soda off the shelf?"

Thomas looked skeptical, but did as he was asked. He quickly returned with the baking soda. He handed it to Esther.

Esther put it back into Thomas' hand and told him, "This lady needs it for her son, so give it to her."

The man's narrow face seemed to get narrower as his mouth flew open, but he said nothing as Thomas went up to his wife and handed her the soda.

"Put a couple of handfuls of the soda in the tub of warm water. That will help the itching and keep the sores clean," Esther told them.

"Thank you so much!" the woman said, tearfully. "I'm so glad we came here. Rebecca said you are a nice lady. Now we know for ourselves."

The man looked relieved, but embarrassed as he got back into the wagon.

Esther heard the baby cry from the cabin. "I have to go, now. Come back to visit when your son is better," she said to the woman. *She won't be back. He won't let her come because of Thomas.*

That night, Jacob read the Bible aloud to Thomas. He read Matthew, chapter 5. As Jacob finished the last verses of the chapter, Thomas asked, "We are kind to white enemies, but we shoot Indian enemies?"

"No, that's not right," Esther told him. "We shoot enemies only when we have no choice. If we didn't shoot those Indians we would be dead. God wants us to protect the lives he gave us."

"Mean words are bad," Thomas said.

"We don't have to be like that man and use mean words back at him," Jacob told him.

Thomas looked thoughtful. He went back to his usual quiet self, and went to bed.

The next week Esther started to write another letter. She was so tired that she was having trouble forming the sentences. *I don't know if they got the first letter. What should I tell them? I want to say so much. I'll just go to bed. Maybe tomorrow the words will come. God, tell my mother I love her and I miss her.*

The next day was hot, but Esther had to add wood to the fire to make supper. She opened the windows as wide as possible to let the heat out of the room. She heard the noise of horses and a wagon a long way off. She saw nothing when she looked out her windows, so she opened the door. Jacob and Thomas were gone to town, so she was concerned. At first she thought the covered wagon belonged to the angry man that wasn't polite enough to give his name, but it was not the same wagon. She heaved a sigh of relief when she noticed that Jacob and Thomas were riding along side of the wagon.

She could hear excited talk as they got closer. The voices tended to blend in with the bump and rattle of the wagon. Esther went back to the kitchen to start supper. She decided to make some extra food. Whoever was in that wagon would probably stay for supper.

When Esther poked her head out the door again, she thought she caught the hint of an Irish accent in the voice that called out above the noises of the horses and wagon. *No, it can't be Darby. It sounds like his voice, but why would he leave his job at the hotel and come here?* Esther picked up the baby and stepped out the door. *There's a man and a woman. I can't see the woman's face with her bonnet on. It is Darby! He will have some news. I can hardly wait. I wonder who he married.*

As Darby stopped the team, the woman turned away to jump off the wagon. Jacob said, "Look who I found at the store, looking for the Durham place!"

When the woman finally faced her, Esther yelled so loud that Eve jumped in her arms. "Leah, I can't believe you're here!"

The women hugged each other. Since the baby was in Esther's arms, she was included in the hug. Leah backed away to look at Eve. "Jacob said the baby was a girl," Leah said. "I have such a beautiful niece."

"You got the letter? We were beginning to think the letter got lost."

"We got the letter. That's why we're here."

"You and Darby are married?" Esther asked. "How did you manage to get that one past your mother? Jacob told me you would be a spinster. He didn't think your mother would let anyone near you."

"I would sneak over and have lunch with him at the hotel between classes. When I graduated from normal training he decided to come courting on his day off. He asked my father. When my father gave his permission, my mother complained a lot, but she couldn't stop it."

"Are you just passing through?" Esther asked.

"No, when Darby saw Jacob's letter, he wanted to come here to get land. He said that gold mines run out of gold, but good farming land is forever."

"That is the best news! You have to tell me about everyone," Esther said. "Let's go into the cabin. I have supper started."

"Rebecca sent you a dozen eggs from the store," Leah said, "I left them in the wagon."

Esther noticed a certain darkness come across Leah's face when *telling about everyone* was mentioned. She knew there would be bad news with the good.

Darby was unusually quiet as he looked at Esther. He and Jacob unhitched the team and took the saddles off the horses. As they walked into the cabin, Darby said, "And where would you be gettin' logs like this? It's been a lot of miles between us and straight logs this size."

"We don't know for sure, but we think the former owner had the logs shipped in on wagons," Jacob replied.

Esther and Leah busied themselves with supper. Esther noticed that every time she started to ask about her mother, or Ira or Kara, the subject was changed. She decided to wait until after supper before she pressed the subject.

After everyone had eaten their fill of fresh corn, potatoes and fried rabbit, Esther announced, "Will someone tell me the bad news now?"

Thomas looked about, wide eyed.

Leah and Darby looked at each other. Finally, Leah spoke. "I have been thinking of how to tell you this the whole way here. I just don't know a good way to say it."

Suddenly, Esther knew in her heart what was so hard to tell. She spoke when Leah hesitated and asked, "How did my mother die?"

Darby, Leah and Jacob all stared at her in disbelief. When Leah recovered, she said, "There was a fire at the hotel. Ira, Kara and their little Ira got out safely, but your mother was asleep upstairs in the back room. She didn't get out. One guest also died."

"Did they find her body?" Esther asked. "I want to know if she has a grave I can visit."

"Yes, they found her body. Ira said the body was found below her room. He thinks that she died without waking up. She's in the church yard."

Esther sat in the rocking chair, crying. *I can't tell them about my mother coming to see me after she died. They wouldn't understand. They would think I was addle brained. Maybe someday I'll tell Jacob. That's why Summer called me her angel! My mother came to her, too. We look alike, so she thought my mother's spirit was back to comfort her. My mother said she was fine. I have these wonderful living people here. I'll try to stop crying.*

Esther dried her eyes on her handkerchief. "Tell me about everyone else. What did Ira and Kara do without a hotel?"

Leah answered her. "Mrs. Kinnen took them in. She had room in her house after Harris left for California. The hotel was being rebuilt as we left. Some said Ira had money in the bank. Some said he carried a box of money out. I think he had to get a loan for most of it."

"He didn't have a lot of money saved, because he helped a lot of people," Esther said with the tears returning to her eyes.

"A lot of people are helping him rebuild. The new hotel will be a grand place," Leah said.

Jacob said, "Esther, if we had left you there while we went to California, you would have been in that room with your mother." He stood and put one arm around her as he was holding Eve with the other arm.

"I had so much to do here," Esther barely managed to say. Thomas stood by, looking lost, so Esther drew him close to them. *I haven't lost nearly as much as Thomas has. I wish I could talk to my mother.*

Esther artificially brightened her voice, "I have company tonight," she said. "We have Leah and Darby here with us. I want to talk about happier things. Darby, when it gets light in the morning, we have to show you the beautiful foal that my horse gave birth to the same day Eve was born."

"Leah, I was so angry with Jacob that day. He wouldn't ride to get the midwife because Joy was having her foal. I have so many things to tell you. What can you tell me about everyone else? You can believe me or not, but I have been wondering how your mother is doing. Ask Jacob. We talked about her just last week."

"Wait just a minute!" Leah said. "You aren't letting me answer. My mother moped around after you left, but after the fire she changed some. We shamed her into thinking of her blessings."

"When Darby came to call, she was sweet to him, but she would complain to me that he wasn't the right kind of caller. She thought I should entertain Harris. When he left for California, she stopped complaining so much."

"Harris? I can't believe she liked Harris," Esther said.

"She was impressed that his father was a ship's captain," Leah said. "I suppose no one told her what kind of a man his father really was."

Jacob looked surprised when Leah said that, but he said nothing.

The men went outside for cool air while the women did the dishes. *I think Leah would like to know the rest of the story about Harris. Neither one of us will see him, again. What will it matter if I tell her? I promised my mother I would never tell. Once I break my word, it can never be fixed. We have to talk of something else.*

"Tell me about your wedding, Leah. Did you and Darby have a big wedding?

Leah smiled, "Not as big as yours, but I liked it. It was just right for us. My mother decided I would have the wedding I wanted, even if she didn't approve of the groom."

"Do you remember the woman that took care of Sheriff Gibbs?" Leah asked.

"Yes, I do," Esther said. "She is so pretty."

"She made my wedding cake. She's a very fine baker. Oh! You didn't know they got married."

"Sheriff Gibbs married her? Did his mind improve?" Esther wondered.

"No, his mind is still bad, but they get along well and they have a baby girl," Leah said. "The baby is so cute, and Mr. Gibbs is such a proud father," Leah continued. "He had a seizure near the church one day. Just before the seizure he handed the baby to his wife."

"I sometimes wonder if the man that hit him on the head knows of the damage he caused," Esther said.

"No one ever heard any more about him, or that man that attacked you," Leah said. "They got away, totally."

"I believe God will be their final judge," Esther said. "Nobody gets totally away from God."

Leah thought a moment and said, "I always thought they would be caught, someday."

Esther said, "Maybe they were caught for another crime. I don't think the one that attacked me would change his behavior. He probably did it again. If he did that type of thing in the west where there is no jail, he would be hanged or shot. At one time I thought I could never stop thinking about that time I was attacked, but so much has happened that I don't even think about it any more."

It was later than the usual bedtime when they finally stopped talking. Esther offered the trundle bed in Thomas' room, but they went to the wagon to sleep. "We have a nice bed in the wagon," Leah said.

The next morning, Esther awoke to sounds in the kitchen. She dressed hurriedly. She hadn't seen a need for a making a house coat, so she had to dress before greeting anyone. "Darby, what are you doing?" she asked when she saw him working in the kitchen.

"I'm sorry to be takin' over with what's yours. I couldn't be seein' this stove sittin' here with no person cookin on it. I'm not wantin' to believe it, and I'm thinkin' it's a bit daft that I miss cookin' on a hot stove. That is, with your kind permission."

"You have my permission," Esther told him. "It will be wonderful to taste someone else's cooking. I'll show you how to get to the root cellar. We put the eggs down there to keep cool."

When she pushed the rug out of the way and lifted the door, Darby asked, "Is that the place you'll be hidin' when Indians attack?"

"No, Indians would burn the cabin," Esther told him. "It's better to stay up here and fight. The Indians haven't attacked here. I don't think they will. The root cellar is a good place to hide from wind storms. This fall, we'll put potatoes and carrots and such in here."

"And where would you be gettin' the potatoes and carrots to be puttin' in there?" Darby asked.

"I'll show you the garden after breakfast," Esther said. "You'll have to see the size of the potatoes to believe them. Is Leah still sleeping?"

"She's walkin' about. She wants be out in the cool of the mornin'."

The baby was crying, so Esther went to feed and change her.

Leah came inside when Darby called her in for breakfast. After breakfast, Thomas went outside with the men. As they were washing the dishes, Leah asked, "How can you live in a place where an Indian woman died?"

Esther thought a moment. "Summer asked me to stay here and take care of her son. We would have frozen last winter if it weren't for this cabin keeping us warm. We would have starved if it weren't for the food she raised in her garden. We didn't bring a wagon full of supplies, so we needed this place with a root cellar."

"Didn't you have money to buy food?"

"We had money, but the snow was too deep. We couldn't get to the store. You and Darby are welcome to stay here, but if you want to get your own place ready before winter, you will have to work long and hard."

Leah was silent.

Esther continued to explain, "I don't even think of this place as the place where Summer died. It's where she lived, and now it's our home. People died at the hotel. We cleaned the room and more people stayed in the room."

"I suppose you're right," Leah said. "All this talk of death has me upset."

"This place is right for me," Esther told her. "You'll find a place where you feel at home. I knew right away that this was the place for me. Maybe you don't feel at home in this country now, but you'll see. There is a lot of good land open here. God will show you the right place."

Jacob came into the house. "Darby wants to look at the Johnson place. We're thinkin' the barn could be fixed up good enough to live in for one season. Do you ladies want to ride along?"

Leah laughed, "Well, maybe a barn is the place for me. I can sleep with the horses. I always did like horses."

Jacob looked at both of them, quizzically, as they both laughed. They didn't try to explain. "Women are strange," he said.

"We'll go," Esther said. "It will take a while to get Eve ready." *Leah and I have different thoughts about things. That's okay, we can still be friends.*

As Esther put some of Eve's things in a bag for the short trip, Thomas came into the room. He watched for a moment, and then asked, "Will you go away to your mother's grave?"

"No, Thomas. Someday I would like to go, but it is so far. I can't be away that long. We're just going to the place where you found the horses."

"Father went to his mother's grave," Thomas said, sadly.

"My father didn't have a grave, either," Esther told him. *How do I explain burial at sea to him?* "He was put in a very big water place called the ocean. That's why I wondered about my mother's grave."

"My father told us about the ocean. He said someday he would show us the big water, so big you can't see land on the other side. Caleb didn't believe him."

"My mother's grave is on land by the ocean. When you are a big man, maybe it will be easier to travel there. All of us could go for a visit."

The concerned look left Thomas' face. Esther saw a smile as he turned to go outside.

16

NORMAL TRAINING APPLIED

JACOB HITCHED UP THEIR TEAM TO DRIVE TO the Johnson place. Darby and Leah's wagon was full of things for them to start life on the prairie. Esther peeked into the wagon.

"Leah, you have a cook stove in here!"

"That was Darby's idea. He said we would need it, and there wouldn't be such a nice one in the west."

"It is a nice one. You need a house to put it in," Esther said. "Everything is hard to get here. Someday they'll put a railroad through here, so we can have things shipped in more easily."

"You always were a dreamer," Leah told her. "I can't believe they'll ever get the railroad this far west."

When they drove into the yard at the former Johnson place, there was a surprise waiting for them. A covered wagon sat in the yard. When they drove in, a man came out of the barn. Jacob and Darby walked over to talk to the man.

"He said they are settling there. They plan to live in the barn this winter," Jacob said when he returned.

Esther thought they would be going home, but Jacob turned toward town. "We're going to town?" Esther asked.

Jacob looked back at Leah. "How would you feel about teaching school this fall?" he asked.

"I would like that, but no one hires a married teacher," Leah told him.

"Out here we don't have many teachers. They had a man last year, but he left for California. We'll go talk to Pup. He can call a meeting."

Pup looked surprised to see them. "I understand the town is looking for a teacher," Jacob said. "My sister, here, has her certificate from normal school. She is married, but if you are still providing a home for the teacher, she might be interested in teaching this winter."

"The home is just a room off the school. It's not meant to be a place for a man and his wife. I'll call Rebecca to mind the store. We can give it a look. Maybe it can be made to be a place to keep the cold wind off your backs," Pup said to Darby. "There's some unsettled land just outside of town. If you've a mind to build there for next year, it's not too far to be comin' back and forth."

The room was incredibly small to serve as a kitchen and bedroom, but Leah said, "We can make this do for one winter, can't we, Darby?"

Leah grew up in a big beautiful home. She doesn't know what it's like to live in one room. At least it is a warm place to be for the winter. Their cook stove might keep it too warm.

"It does have what we'll be in need of in the cold of winter," Darby said. "We can leave some of what we need in the wagon."

"I can't promise for the whole town," Pup said. "I'll ask the men hereabouts. They'll have an idea when they can come to a meetin'. I expect we'll know in a week. A teacher that's married can still teach if it's up to me, but you know how some folks are."

"I want to be there when they meet," Jacob said. "I'll check back in a few days. Just be sure we don't keep it hanging till I have to start on the harvest. I'll have no time for meetings, then."

"You and all the rest of 'em. We'll git 'er done," Pup promised.

Jacob drove north of town as they left the store. "I'll show you the land that Pup mentioned." Just outside of town the river flowed crooked, so some of the land was low. Darby and Leah walked around while Esther stayed in the wagon to feed Eve.

Darby was silently thoughtful till they were all in the wagon, again. "I'm thinkin' that bit of land would be just what the two of us will be needin'," he said, finally.

Jacob said, "It's not the best of farming land."

Darby smiled, knowingly. "I'm just thinkin' I'll go back to the cookin'. It's more families I see comin' in and out of town, and no place to sit and eat a little. Soldiers from the fort may want some good food."

"Building a place like that will take a lot of work. I'll help you build if you help with the harvest."

"Help with takin' in the grain is no more than right, to my way o' thinkin'," Darby said.

When they were back at the cabin, Esther had a chance to talk to Leah alone. "Leah," she asked, "is there some reason I can't teach Thomas to read? The only book we have is the Bible. He learns his letters and some words on the slate, but when I show him words in the Bible, he can't read them."

Leah nodded knowingly, as Esther was talking. She asked, "Does Thomas see things well at a distance?"

"He recognizes people a long way off. I can barely tell a bearded man from a woman in a bonnet, and he knows who it is."

"Thomas probably can't see the fine print in the Bible. If he wears spectacles, he will most likely be able to learn."

"I don't know where we have to go to find spectacles," Esther said. "Maybe Pup will have some idea how we can get some. If that's holding him back, we'll have to get some."

The meeting was not as Esther had hoped. The men went into the meeting while the women and children stayed outside. Some women brought their needlework. *It's our children's education, too! Why can't we be a part of the decisions? I'm grateful to have women to visit with, but I want to be in there.*

Leah stayed outside, pacing while she waited for someone to call her in to the meeting.

Fiona told her, "You're worse than a father waitin for the birth. I'll tell you what I tell them. Save that walkin' for when there's work to be done."

"I can't help it. I want to teach. I thought I would have to give it up when Darby and I were married. Now that I might have a chance to teach after all, I realized how much I want it."

"Women have always gave it all up for love," Fiona said. "Sometimes it's too late to get it back when you know you still want it."

Esther said, "Fiona wants to learn to read."

Fiona was aghast. "Listen to you, now. Like I would have a head for learnin' at my age!"

Leah looked surprised and then said, "We all keep learning every day. Sometimes life makes us learn hard lessons. Sometimes we choose what we learn. **Choose** learning to read."

One of the men came to the doorway and called, "Mrs. O'Halloran, we would like you to come in now."

Fiona stared after Leah as she walked into the schoolroom. "Do you think I really could learn to read?" she asked Esther. Before Esther could answer, she said, "When would I get time for that?"

"You take a little time every day," Esther told her. "You will always wonder if you could have done it if you don't try. Your children are old enough to do a lot for themselves. They do a lot of work when you are gone delivering a baby, so each of them can do a little more, while you learn to read and write."

"If I learned to read, I wouldn't have to ask someone else to read for me all the time. Some of the things I buy in a can look alike," Fiona said, almost to herself. "I trust Pup to give me the right change, but I would like to learn to count money, too. I hope those men in there have their heads on straight. They have to hire that young woman. Our children need a woman like her. I never thought I'd find another woman like yourself that is so wise at such a young age."

As time went on Esther and Fiona impatiently stared at the door of the school. Thomas came up to Esther and asked, "Is there an enemy in there?"

Esther smiled at him and said, "We want them to hire Leah for a teacher. There may be some men that don't want to hire her for a teacher."

"She's going to be my teacher," Thomas said. "One man didn't want me there, but the man with the sick boy said I should learn to be like a white man, so I don't go back to Indian ways."

"How did you hear all that?" Fiona asked him.

"I went into the back room. They have the back doors open." Thomas looked at Esther and said, "You said I should stay close by where I can hear you call."

"You're not in trouble, Thomas, but it is impolite to listen to people talk when they don't know you are listening," Esther told him.

"Is it impolite to say I can't learn to read?" Thomas asked.

"That's impolite, and the person who said that is an ignorant so and so!" Fiona told him. "You will show them all that you can learn to read and cipher, too!"

I will get those spectacles for Thomas! We may have to go a long ways to find them, but we will find them. We have to prove those people wrong. Just because he's half Indian doesn't mean he is slow!

Leah came out smiling. Esther forced a big smile when Leah said that she was hired. She looked at Jacob as she gave Leah a hug. She could see some of the same anger on his face that she felt, but he, too, forced a smile for his sister.

This is the first time Jacob has had to deal with the hate for Thomas. People don't call him names when he is with Thomas.

"We have to talk to Pup about getting some spectacles for Thomas before we leave town," Esther told Jacob. When Jacob looked at her quizzically, she added, "Leah says he probably can't see the fine print in the Bible well enough to read it."

Pup walked out of the school as Esther was speaking. "What is that you say? I heard my name, said, but wait till I get there to start sayin' good things."

"Thomas needs a pair of spectacles to see fine print," Esther told him. "He can't learn to read if he can't see the words."

"We can't have anybody sayin' that smart boy can't read." Pup said, in a voice that was louder than his usual loud voice. "Come on over to the store. I ordered in some spectacles for some folks, but they never came for them. Spectacles don't go bad on me, so I kept them in stock. We'll give 'em a try."

The spectacles looked strange on Thomas' face, so Esther stifled a laugh when Pup put them on his face.

"I don't like them," Thomas said as he looked around.

"They aren't for looking far away," Leah told him. She asked Pup, "Do you have any books or anything with fine print?"

Thomas started to take the spectacles off his face, but he stopped when Esther said, "Leave them on till we find something for you to look at up close."

Pup put a book on the counter. Leah told Thomas to look at the letters in the book. "Can you find an *A* for me?" She asked.

Thomas pointed and said, "Is that an A?"

"That sure is!" Pup said.

"There's lots of letters in there!" Thomas said, excitedly.

"Take the spectacles off and look," Esther said.

"I can't see the letters, now," Thomas said. "I need to put these on to see the letters!"

"Take good care of those," Jacob told him. "They are easy to break. Put them in your shirt pocket for when you need them. Leave them at home when we go out to the field."

Thomas nodded.

When they arrived at home, Thomas went to the Bible, put on his spectacles and opened it. He smiled, broadly. "I can see the letters, now," he said. "Leah, will you teach me to read tomorrow?"

Thomas looked disappointed when everyone laughed.

Darby told Thomas, "It'll be takin' a lot of your tomorrows to be learnin' the readin'. And then there's the numbers. Oh, the figurin', that's a hard one. When ya think you'll be done larnin', they throw some more at ya again."

Thomas looked bewildered. "It takes a long time to learn all that," Jacob told him.

"I know all my letters, so it won't take long to learn words," Thomas said, confidently.

The adults all smiled as they looked at each other.

In bed that night, Esther asked Jacob, "Who was it that didn't want Thomas to go to school?"

"How did you hear about that?" Jacob said, incredulously. "Did you just pick that out of the air, too? Leah wasn't in the room yet."

"No, I didn't just know that. Thomas was in the back room, listening. He heard someone say he didn't need to go to school because he couldn't learn."

"I wasn't going to tell him that," Jacob said.

"Who was it?" Esther repeated.

"I don't know if I should tell you. Do you promise not to shoot him?"

Esther poked her husband, playfully, on the shoulder. "You know I wouldn't shoot him. That wouldn't change any minds to the right way of thinking!"

Jacob laughed. "Oh, that's right, you would shoot his horse."

"I promise, I won't even shoot his horse," Esther said as she poked Jacob in the shoulder again.

Jacob's voice became serious as he said, "It was Cyrus Hunt that spoke up. I could tell some of the others agreed with him."

"They will find out that Thomas can learn as well as their children do," Esther told him.

At harvest time, Esther and Leah stayed in the house with Eve, while everyone else went to the fields. Some of the neighbors were there to help with the harvest. Esther made apple pies the night before. She bought apples Rebecca had taken in trade for other food. The apples were from the Johnson place. She saved seed from the apples, hoping she, too, could raise apples. Corn meal muffins were made from last year's corn ground by hand in the winter. She dug new potatoes and picked green beans from the garden. Fresh meat was hard to come by at this time of year. The neighbors who raised hogs would butcher later in the fall. The same was true of the beef they raised. Jacob was busy with the harvest, so he didn't have time for hunting. Before the harvest began, Esther found a roasting hen that a neighbor was willing to trade for the promise of beef they would butcher later in the fall. She got up early to butcher the chicken.

Esther and Leah gathered the dirty dishes from the meal when everyone went back to the fields. Eve was crying and wanted to be fed. Esther picked her up.

"Leah, just sit a minute with me while I feed Eve. You have been on your feet since before dawn."

Leah did not object. She sat in Jacob's easy chair. "I don't know if I'll want to get back to work after sitting in this. Do you realize that food took us all day to prepare, and the men ate it all in just a few minutes?"

"Not only that, but it took a lot of work in the garden to raise the vegetables. I'm glad we don't have to do this every day," Esther told her. "I am thankful you were here to help today. I couldn't have done it alone."

Leah and Darby moved into their room as soon as harvest was over. Esther was sad and glad at the same time to watch them go. *It was nice to have more help with all the work. I have become accustomed to having more alone time, though.*

Later that fall, Thomas rode off to school on Jacob's horse. Esther watched him ride toward town in the cool of the morning. *I hope he'll be all right. The other children might treat him badly, because of the way their parents feel. I have too much work to do to worry about that all day. God, help Thomas show them what a wonderful person he is.*

When Thomas returned, he had a smile on his face. Esther asked, "How was your first day in school?"

"It was a good day, but I have to go back tomorrow," Thomas said brightly.

Esther tried not to laugh out loud. She put on a serious face as she told him, "I went to school every winter for eleven years."

"It won't take me that long to learn," he answered confidently.

Esther decided to allow Thomas to realize for himself that there was a lot to learn. *His world has been this prairie and what he has learned when his father read the Bible. He and I both have a lot to learn.*

17

BUILDING FAMILY AND MORE

THE WAGON APPROACHING FROM THE SOUTHWEST WAS AN unusual sight. In the nine years they had lived there, a wagon had never come from the direction of the Indian Territory. Esther looked up from her washboard to check on the progress of the wagon as she worked to finish the last piece of laundry. She wrung out Jacob's pants and hurried to add them to the rest of the family laundry on the clothesline. The clothesline barely held their wash. The hot August sun would bake them dry, even if they weren't spread out as well as they could be.

"Eve!" she called. *She's probably reading. Jacob and Thomas spoil her, buying her new books to read. She would spend the whole summer reading if I let her.*

"She's in the outhouse," their second daughter, Millie, said.

"Did she take a book with her?" Esther asked.

"I don't know." Millie said.

I suppose she hid it in her skirt. I don't know why she reads in there. The only light shines in through the cracks and knot holes, and it stinks worse than usual in there in August. She knows she's supposed to be out here helping me.

"Eve! We're getting company!" Esther called out.

Eve came out quickly. After looking toward town, she said, "I don't see anyone." She glared at her mother as though she had been tricked.

"Look that way," Esther said as she pointed.

"Nobody lives that way but Indians," Eve declared.

Esther and the girls were watching so intently they didn't notice Jacob and Thomas approaching from the other way on horseback, until Thomas' horse whinnied, startling them. Jacob and Thomas stayed on their horses, staring at the same covered wagon.

Esther saw that there were two white men on the wagon seat. Behind her, she heard

Thomas say, "One of them is Elliot."

Esther stared at Thomas. "You barely saw Elliot nine years ago," she said, "How is it that you remember him?"

"I remember. He was afraid of me," Thomas said.

"Why was he afraid of you?" Eve asked him, as she pushed her blonde hair out of her face.

Thomas shrugged.

"Thomas was sick," Esther told her. "Elliot was afraid of catching smallpox from him."

"Smallpox?" Eve said "Why didn't Thomas die?"

Even Thomas was looking at Esther for the answer to that question. "He must have been able to fight it off."

The wagon was very close before Esther could see that Elliot was driving the wagon. Beside him sat a man with his hat on and an untrimmed red beard that Esther didn't recognize. He called out a loud, "Hello!"

It sounds like Harris! Can it be him?

As the men descended, Esther noticed the wagon seat was cushioned with sheepskin. *I think I won't mention the sheepskin. Not in front of the children, anyway. They wouldn't understand how well I know this man. He is still skinny. California food didn't fatten him.*

"It's been a long time between visits, friend!" Jacob declared.

"That it has!" Elliot agreed. "You remember Harris Kinnen, don't you?"

"I say, he looks familiar!" Jacob declared. "It's been a long time since I saw him in school. Welcome to both of you!"

Esther's thoughts went back to what her mother had told her so many years ago. *I never did tell Jacob about Harris. I didn't think I would ever see him again.*

Jacob said, "You remember Thomas, and these are our girls, Eve and Millie."

"This is the same boy?" Elliot asked. "I didn't think he'd live." Elliot shook Thomas' offered hand. "You were a sick little boy the last time I saw you."

"I believe you two would like a home cooked meal," Esther said.

Harris said, "We are da. . . , excuse me, we **are** tired of trail food. I haven't had a good meal since I left home."

"We may not have all the food your mother had available, but we have some frying chickens running around here this year. If someone will catch one or two, I'll do my best at cooking."

Thomas got back on his horse to look around. He rode Joy's foal, the spotted horse. "I'll get the chickens," he said, as he rode off.

Usually, the chicken would be caught at night on the roost, and kept in an overturned box, so the chicken's crop would be empty for butchering, but this was a special occasion. Esther got a pail and a potato fork before going to the garden for potatoes and other vegetables. The men unhitched the horses and pumped water for them. Esther asked Eve to pick corn. The first planting was already too ripe for roasting ears, but they planted some later to have fresh corn longer.

As Esther put the food on the table she asked, "I want to know how the two of you found each other and if you were able to find gold in California?"

Harris answered, "We just ran into each other in the trading post. When we got to talking about our claims, we found out we were just a stone's throw away from each other. We were some of the few that found gold. We both decided we didn't want to stay single all our lives, so we decided to go back east far enough to find a wife. All the women in California are newborn or married."

After the meal, everyone sat still to visit as the air cooled. Harris suddenly got up, got hot water from the tea kettle and washed his hands in the basin. "Esther, I have something for you in the wagon," he said.

Harris brought in a large paper, rolled, and protected with a cloth. He held the paper open for Esther to see. After gazing at the paper, tears came to Esther's eyes. It was an ink drawing of their wedding. Her mother, Ira, Kara and Jacob's parents were in the drawing.

"Did you draw this, Harris?" Esther asked.

"Yes, I did, but I didn't think it would make you cry," Harris said.

Jacob was looking over Esther's shoulder. "When did you do this?" he asked.

"I did it at home, right after the wedding," Harris said. "When my mother saw it, she told me I had to bring it to you, so she found a box to carry it in. This went with me in the wagon to California, in case I could find you there."

Jacob asked, "Did you leave before the fire?"

Eliot and Harris answered at once by saying, "What fire?"

"Esther's mother was killed when the hotel burned," Jacob said.

Harris looked at Esther, "I'm sorry," he said, "Your mother was a good friend to my mother."

"I am crying because you have brought a precious remembrance of all of us on that day," Esther managed to say. "I can't thank you enough for this." Esther washed and dried her hands, too, so she could hold the paper. Thomas, Eve and Millie crowded close to see it. "Harris, you are very talented," Esther said as she held the drawing.

Harris looked at Esther. "My mother said I owed you this."

Jacob looked at Harris and Esther for an explanation.

Esther turned to Jacob, "I'll explain, later," she told him. "I feel like a queen to have a portrait of our wedding. Very few people have that. We have to show this to Leah and Darby!"

"Leah and Darby?" Harris asked.

"Leah and Darby were married," Esther explained. "They live in the town north of here. They have two boys."

"We have to go to town, anyway," Elliot said. "We have to find someone called the Strong Medicine Woman. Do you know where we can find her?"

Thomas grinned. Jacob laughed out loud.

"He's serious," Harris said. "We were going to go around the Indian land to avoid trouble, but the owner of the trading post said we might be able to go straight through, if we asked the Indians for safe passage."

Elliot continued, "You know how I am about traveling extra miles, so we asked some of the Indians hanging around the store about safe passage. They left to talk to the chief. When they came back, they said we could have safe passage to see the Strong Medicine Woman. We have to tell her that they gave us safe passage. We asked the owner of the trading post, and he said that he heard about this woman. She drove out a soldier who was threatening a tribe that she protected. There was another tribe that attacked the same tribe. She killed some of the braves and the rest of the tribe got sick. The man at the trading post said we had better find that woman if we took the short way, or we would be killed."

Jacob was still smiling as he said, "Elliot, I told you before we started west, I was marrying a very special woman."

After an initial look of surprise, Elliot said, "I should have known. Esther is the Strong Medicine Woman."

"They weren't just playing a trick on us?" Harris asked.

Elliot said, "Harris, you saw the Indians following till we got close to this cabin."

Eve broke her polite silence to say, "My mother didn't do those things."

Esther quickly said, "I got the credit for giving them the measles. The truth is that they were able to kill the River Tribe, because the whole tribe had the measles. They got the measles from the River Tribe. Indians have no immunity to the diseases that white people had as children. God is protecting us by letting them believe these things."

Elliot looked at Eve and said, "Did your mother tell you the story of how she shot the horse thieves?"

"No, she didn't," Eve said with a tone that suggested she was ready to hear. She looked at her mother with questioning eyes.

"You may as well tell her," Esther said, as Elliot was looking in her direction in a questioning manner. "You already opened up the bees' nest."

Thomas, too, was very attentive as Elliot began the story. "It finally got cool enough for me to get some sleep when I heard gun shots. Esther saw some dirty thief takin her horse and she shot 'im. They were yellin about shootin us if we went for our guns."

"Didn't any of you get shot?" Eve asked.

"Your mother shot two of 'em before we even got up out of our bed rolls. They got out of there."

"Why did you shoot them?" Eve asked Esther.

Harris spoke up, and said, "If a dirty thief steals your horse when you're in the wilderness, he's takin' your life away. That's why they hang horse thieves."

"They called out that they were planning to shoot us if we woke up," Jacob said. "They didn't see your mother move. I have always believed they planned to steal our horses first, and then when we were forced to leave our saddles and most of our supplies behind, they could pick them up without any risk."

"Are the two of you going all the way to the east coast?" Esther asked. "If you are, we should send a letter to Jacob's parents and to Kara and Ira."

"We'll take the letter. Harris wants to show his mother that he's still alive," Elliot said.

"We both left our mothers alone," Esther told Harris.

"My mother wasn't alone," Harris said. "A man she knew in England before I was born came to find her. They were married before I left."

Esther and Harris exchanged a knowing glance. When Harris looked at Jacob, he asked, "She really didn't tell you, did she?"

Jacob looked uneasy. "Leah told us about the names you called her. My mother thought it was true."

"It was **not** true. I don't know how I could have done that to her. My mother told me about her father dying on the way to America on the ship. Now my mother is married to the man she first loved. He came looking for her after his first wife died."

"What a romantic story!" Esther said. "Are they happy together?"

"They were happy when I left them. I am looking forward to seeing them, but they don't need me there."

"A mother always needs her children," Esther told him.

The two men went to town with them to visit with Leah and Darcy. During that time the whole story of the Indian killing was told. When they went to the store, Pup told the story in his inimitable fashion.

The two spent a few days helping Jacob in the oat field, shocking the oats.

When the time came for the two men to leave, Esther almost cried. Still, she was glad to send the letters, knowing they would be carried to each person with care.

After the harvest was over, there were a few weeks of good weather. The unbearable heat of summer was waning to warm afternoon breezes and cool evenings. There was just enough cool rain to keep the grass green.

Esther was wondering about the words she would use to tell Jacob they would be having their third child. *I think Jacob will be surprised this time. We could use more space. Maybe Jacob will agree to add another room onto the cabin. He built a granary during the summer, before harvest. He built the chicken coop. Maybe, somehow, there would be time to build a room for Eve and Millie in the spring after planting and before the haying. The baby can sleep with Thomas if he's a boy, or Eve and Millie if she's a girl.*

Esther heard a wagon. She went to the door and looked out. Jacob was driving in from the field, but she was hearing another wagon. She walked partway out the door and turned her head to see someone approaching in a wagon she didn't recognize. *Thomas is with Jacob, so he can't use his eyes to tell me who this is or if they have weapons ready. I have to stop thinking that way. I am safe here. I shouldn't mistrust people just because they are strangers. Jacob still takes his gun to the field in case of Indian trouble. I'll put my gun on and cover it with my apron.*

Esther heard Jacob calling out to the people in the wagon as though he knew them. She slipped off her gun and hung it on the bed post. She quickly brushed her hair into place. The men's voices she heard were talking about driving the wagon around so the horses could drink without unhitching them. Esther put the water on to make coffee and put wood in the fire. *I wonder if these people will be afraid to come into the cabin. It's been more than nine years, but some people still think they will get smallpox if they come into this cabin.*

Esther couldn't take the suspense any longer, so she went to look out the door. She saw two strangers still talking with Jacob. Thomas was seeing to the horses, letting them loose to graze.

When Jacob saw her, he said, "Come on in and meet my wife."

The men walked in, almost reluctantly. Esther noticed a surprised look on their faces when they saw her. She saw another surprised look when they saw Eve and Millie. *The men are wondering how two white people have an Indian son. They are, at least, too polite to ask.*

"Esther, this is Mr. Olson and Mr. Jacobson," Jacob said. He had a sly smile on his face. "This is my wife, Esther," he told them.

"Coffee will be ready in a few minutes," Esther told them. She noticed the sly smile had not left Jacob's face. She stood staring at Jacob to send him the message that he should explain to her why these men came here. His sly smile continued as he seemed to be enjoying her curiosity too much to end it.

Esther went to add the coffee grounds to the boiling water. She had nothing baked to serve with the coffee. The cabin would heat up too much at this time of year, so she liked to let the fire die down in the afternoon. *If Jacob knew we had company coming, he should have told me. I would have baked something.*

Mr. Olson said, "We should look at the building site. Do you plan to build here by the existing well?"

Esther could not speak. They had not talked of building a house in years. *I thought this cabin was the only house I would get.*

"Esther, where do you want the new house built?" Jacob said. "These men are here to help us plan and build the new house I promised you."

"A two story house?" Esther asked, incredulously, as she looked toward both men and Jacob.

"Is that what I promised you?" Jacob asked. He looked at Esther and realized he had teased her enough. "We'll build it as big as you want."

"Can we really afford to do it?"

"That's what we're here for," Mr. Olson said as he set out some drawings.

Thomas had a strange look on his face as he looked at the plans with Jacob and Esther.

Later, when the men had left, Esther asked Thomas, "Don't you want a new house?"

"People walk over my head," he said.

"I don't understand," Esther told him.

It was difficult to see Thomas blush, but he definitely blushed. "I don't want to live in that house," he said. "People will walk over my head."

"Would you like a new house without an upstairs?" Esther asked.

Thomas nodded. He had a plaintive look on his face that Esther had rarely seen.

Jacob spoke up, "Did your mother tell you about walking over people's heads?"

"She said it's very bad to walk over someone's head," Thomas told Jacob.

Jacob went back to the plans. "Would it work if your bedroom was next to the kitchen? If you sleep where there was no upstairs over it, like the kitchen, would you like that plan?"

Thomas looked relieved. "I would like that," he said.

"This will be your home, too, Thomas," Jacob said. "Esther has always wanted a two story house. This way, you can both get what you want. A man has to remember to follow his mother's teaching."

Eve said, "I want my own bedroom. I'm tired of sharing my room with Millie," Eve said.

Esther gave Eve a stern look.

"You don't have to tell me," Eve said. "I know. You only had one room to live in when you were young."

"Not only that, but we have a better place to live in than many of the settlers," Esther said.

"We'll build the house as fast as we can, but it may take two years or more," Jacob said. "We have to bring most of the supplies in by wagon. We may not get the foundation started before winter."

That night when the children were asleep, Esther asked, "Can we really pay for a big house?"

"Elliot gave us a share of his gold. With that gold, and the cattle and horses we sold last year, we have enough to build the house," Jacob told her. "We will have to help build it, but the materials will be paid for. I told Elliot he didn't owe us anything, but he insisted. He said not to tell you till after they left. He said there would be no gold if it weren't for you. Harris gave us some gold, too. He said something strange. He said to thank you for all you did for his mother, even though it meant some people believed his words. He said that after they were gone, you could tell me."

"Why didn't you ask till now?"

"I wanted to surprise you with the news after the men got here," Jacob said.

Esther was thoughtfully quiet for a moment. "Elliot couldn't tell me to my face."

"Do you know what Harris meant?" Jacob persisted.

"Yes, I understand exactly what he was saying. Mr. Kinnen wasn't his father. His mother married for the first time after Harris was born. My mother and I knew this."

"My mother would feel foolish, if she knew that," Jacob said. "She wanted Leah to take up with him."

"You can't **ever** write that to her, Jacob! It would hurt Mary Kinnen so much to have her secret told. She is a nice woman that made a big mistake when she was young. My mother made me promise not to tell, so I never did. Harris was saying we could know, but he doesn't want his mother hurt."

"I would never let her know. I was just saying she … well she has a way of judging others without knowing them. I'm glad to know I married a woman that accepts others for the good in them." Jacob kissed his wife.

Esther lay quietly thinking for a moment. "Jacob, why is it that men can make mistakes when they are young and their mistakes are just considered to be a young man's folly, but women are forever fallen women?"

Jacob was thoughtful, and then asked, "How do you expect me to answer that? Only God knows the answer to a question like that."

Esther changed the subject. "We'll have a new baby before spring. I was going to ask if we could add to the cabin, but I like the idea of starting a new house," Esther said.

When Jacob said nothing, Esther asked, "Were you surprised about the baby?"

"Well, I knew it was likely before the house was built."

"You were surprised!"

"A little bit," Jacob admitted.

"I wonder if the baby will be a girl or a boy. We have two girls, so a boy would be nice."

"Whatever God gives us will be fine," Jacob said. "We have a son named Thomas."

"You're right, but he doesn't have our last name," Esther observed.

"We won't change that," Jacob said. "He needs to keep his father's name. His father had a good name. Thomas is the only one left to carry the name."

Esther lay in thoughtful silence for a moment, and then she said, "Our name isn't on this land. Should we build a house on it?"

"We're building on Thomas' land. He won't make us leave," Jacob told her. "When parents die, their children inherit the land. It's already Thomas' land, or maybe I should say we live on God's land. We just use it while we're here."

"I see what you mean," Esther told him. "We have to trust in God's providence."

18

GOLDEN DAY

As SHE LOOKED ABOUT, ESTHER KNEW THERE WAS no reason for the way she felt. She had all the things she had hoped for so many years ago. The beautiful new house was finished, as Jacob had promised. It was many times the size of the cabin she lived in when she first came to the place she called Dish Land. The kitchen was in a room on the east end of the house, where the cooking fire wouldn't heat up the rest of the rooms in the summer.

Now that the house was built, she and Jacob enjoyed Sunday visitors often. During the week, the ladies would, on occasion, come to her house for quilting, as she was the one with a large enough room. She taught the younger ladies the fancy stitches she learned in school.

This day Leah came to visit, unexpectedly. She was wearing a dress she usually wore when she taught school. Now that her children were older she had been asked to teach again.

Esther and Leah sat in the dining room to have their coffee, so as to avoid the heat of the kitchen. They talked of incidental things while Esther waited for Leah to explain the visit. It wasn't Sunday. Leah usually brought someone with her.

Finally Leah began to speak, seriously, "Esther, I'm here as a teacher, because I have been asked to speak to you. This is not my idea. Some members of the school board don't want Thomas to spend any time at the school now that he is not a student there." Leah spoke quickly, as though the words would burn her tongue if she held them in too long.

"He was tutoring some of the children who were behind in their studies last winter. Why don't they like that?"

"They said I was hired for the job, not him."

"That's not the real reason." Esther said. Her tone and demeanor made it a question.

"They did mention that Thomas is a young man. Some of the parents don't want him around their young ladies."

Esther stared at Leah. After a pause, she said, "Leah, I don't know how to fight this hatred for Thomas. He is not just some Indian. He is a gentleman. I have always known that he may have a difficult time finding a wife, but he will not harm the girls at school."

"I know that," Leah said. "I have to admit there was a time when even I wondered if he could be civilized. I thought if I could teach him, then everyone would know what a good teacher I really am. I was wrong. He was one of my best students. It wasn't my brilliant teaching. He was a brilliant student."

"Leah, I wish I could just take my gun and shoot the hate away. I hoped other people would eventually see what you and I see. Thomas is nothing like the Indians that kill white settlers and soldiers. Maybe, someday, people will be proud to say they have Indian blood in them."

Leah laughed. Esther glowered at her for laughing. Leah stopped laughing long enough to say, "I was going to say you are a **dreamer**. Then I remembered how many times I have told you that. You told me that someday I may teach in the west. You told me that someday the railroad would bring supplies west. I didn't believe there would ever be a railroad this far west."

"Jacob told me about the railroad coming through Iowa. That will be wonderful for all of us. I had forgotten I even said that," Esther said. "I am a dreamer. Lately, my dreams seem to be lost in dark clouds. I think the railroad will be finished a long time before people accept Thomas for what he is."

"Do you want me stay long enough to tell Thomas he can't help me at school this winter?" Leah asked.

"I will see that he knows. They haven't started the harvest. Maybe I'll ask Jacob if he can explain it to him. I don't know how to tell him that some Christians don't accept another Christian because he looks like an enemy."

"When you say it that way, I wonder how we can explain it to him, too," Leah said.

As Leah left, Esther considered how she could even tell Jacob that Thomas was not wanted at the school. *Why don't people even try to understand Thomas?* Esther remembered the time Fiona's niece came with the ladies that came to tie a quilt. As she was shown about the house, she had commented that Thomas lived in the servant's quarters. When they returned to the parlor, Esther tried to explain why Thomas didn't want to be upstairs, or under the upper floor. Everyone stared blankly. One of the ladies said that if he were truly a Christian, he would no longer believe that. Esther pointed out that many people hold beliefs that are not Christian. Mr.

Olson carries a rabbit's foot, and the lady herself wore a *lucky* coin on a chain about her neck. She could remember saying, "Thomas recalls so little of either of his parents that we couldn't ask him to deny what his mother told him about people walking over the heads of others." The ladies nodded, but she could tell they still didn't understand. Now the townspeople were afraid to have Thomas near their daughters. *How can I fight the awful unreasonable hate?*

Esther went upstairs to her bedroom and sat by her vanity. The house was built higher on the dish than the cabin had been. She could look out to see their cattle and horses, grazing contentedly. She could also see the fenced-in fields of grain above the dish.

She thought of each one of their family: *Eve, my first born, Millicent (named after my mother) and Olivia (named after my mother-in-law). Thomas is a young man.*

Today, Thomas and Jacob had gone to town, again, as they often did during this time before the harvest. They would just tell her they were leaving and go. *Don't they ever consider that I may want something from town? I might even want to ride along. When they get home I'll tell them how inconsiderate they are.*

Noisy arguing interrupted Esther's thoughts. The youngest two girls came into her bedroom. "Mother!" Olivia said, indignantly. "Tell Millie to leave my things alone! She has stolen my brush!"

"My brush is gone! I can't find it anywhere!" Millie countered. "I'll put her brush right back when I finish brushing my hair."

"She gets her dirty brown hair in it!" Olivia said as she pushed her own blonde hair back from her face.

Esther reached into a drawer in the vanity. She pulled out the wooden comb Jacob had made for her, years before. Some of the teeth were broken. She could still see the stains from the gun oil.

"Oh, mother!" Millie said. You don't expect me to use that old thing! Why don't you throw it out?"

"Your father made it for me. It was a wonderful gift." Esther said. "I was so happy to have something to take the rats out of my hair."

"Are you going to tell us that story again?" Olivia asked. "We shouldn't have to do without a brush because you did."

Esther raised her voice. "You girls have so much! I can't believe you are complaining about sharing a brush till we can get to town?! Millie, I want you to let Olivia know when you need to use her brush. Olivia, share with your sister! You are lucky to have sisters! When I think of the time I spent without seeing another woman! Esther lowered her voice as she looked at Olivia, "Millie's hair is not any dirtier than yours. I don't want to hear any more fighting over a little thing like a brush!"

The girls were quiet, but unrepentant. Millie began brushing her hair hard, as she stared at Olivia. Olivia left the room in a huff.

"Please pull the hair out of the brush before you give it back to Olivia, and thank her for the use of it," Esther told Millie, controlling her voice to keep the anger out of it. Millie nodded, reluctantly, and angrily stomped out of the room.

Those girls don't appreciate what I went through. Nobody does. Even Jacob doesn't act like he understands and he went through it with me. Thomas used to be afraid that I would leave him. Now he leaves me and goes off with Jacob. I protected Thomas and cared for him. The townspeople don't even want Thomas around. God, why do I feel so miserable? How long do I have to wait for some sign that we did the right thing by staying here? We might have taken Thomas and gone to California. I know we would have found gold. We would be rich now. I could hire a maid to help me cook and clean this big house. We got some gold twice. God, what kind of gold would get rid of these awful feelings?

Esther went downstairs and started to go to the kitchen to work on supper, but decided to walk out onto the porch. Maybe the fresh air would help her. She could see Jacob and Thomas in the distance, riding toward home. Even at that distance she could see that their pants were brighter blue than when they left. *They bought new, readymade pants in town. I don't suppose they even gave it a thought that I need a dress length, so I can make a new dress. If they had only given me time to ask, I would have told them.*

Esther was watching the riders so intently that she didn't hear the horse and buggy approach from the east till it was nearly there. "Whoa!" the driver of the fancy little buggy called out. When it came to a stop, an old man with stooped shoulders got out. His grey beard was neatly trimmed. His thin frame was dressed in an expensive suit. As he put one foot on the step, he removed his hat to reveal thinning grey hair.

"Ma'am, I'm not sure I have the right place," he said. I'm looking for the place where some people raised a part Indian boy with the last name of Martinson. I was at the place once, but it just had a log cabin on it, then."

Esther pointed behind the man, "You can see my husband coming with the boy, now."

The man turned and intently watched the approaching men. "That's my grandson," he said. A tear made its way down the man's cheek. As the man watched north, the lowering sun's rays made the tear look gold in color. "Is he Caleb, or Thomas?" he asked.

"Thomas," Esther said. She began to consider a polite way to ask the burning questions in her mind.

The man spoke in a raspy, emotional voice, "I told my son that I disowned him for marrying an Indian woman. He wrote me about the children, but I never answered him. When I heard they all died of smallpox, I knew what an awful mistake I had made. I heard somebody had settled on this place. I didn't know my grandson was alive till now. There was a man telling me about an educated half breed that wore spectacles. When the man said that his last name was the same as mine, I knew he had to be my grandson."

As he spoke, the man kept his eyes focused toward Thomas. "I don't know how I can thank the two of you for raising Thomas. He is the only one I have left in this world. I can't begin to tell you how I felt when I learned my grandson is alive. I hope he can forgive an old man."

*A golden tear of joy on the face of this old man is my gold. Forgive **me**, God. I have had the love of a family, including Thomas, for the years this man was alone. Thank you, God, for showing me the gold in this day.*

ISBN 142518309-3